"We Get Married And Raise The Baby Together."

To his chagrin, Jenna laughed. Not just laughed but snorted and snuffled with it, as if she couldn't contain her mirth at all.

"It's not so impossible to think of, is it?" he demanded.

"Impossible? It's ridiculous, Dylan. We barely even know one another."

He nodded in agreement. "True. That's something easily rectified."

All humor fled from her face. "You're serious, aren't you?"

"Never more so."

"No. It would never work. Not in a million years."

"Why not? We already know we're—" he paused a moment for effect, his eyes skimming her face, her throat and lower "—compatible."

"Great sex isn't the sole basis for a compatible marriage," she protested.

"It's a start," he said, his voice deepening.

* * *

Expecting the CEO's Child is a Dynasties: The Lassiters novel—A Wyoming legacy of love, lies and redemption!

* * *

If you're on Twitter,
tell us what you think of Harlequin Desire!
#harlequindesire

Dear Reader,

We've all heard stories about "love rats" and people who scam others in the name of "love," and it got me thinking, what happens to the people left behind—particularly, the families of the scammers? How painful must it have been to be put under a spotlight that was not of your making and even to be tarred with the same brush, especially if you weren't involved? How precious would privacy be to you, and how hard would you work to rebuild your life? And so the character of Jenna Montgomery was born in my mind.

Of course, for every privacy-seeking person, there's one who courts publicity. That person who thrives on being known and using that notoriety to further their business—in this case, Dylan Lassister, celebrity chef and new CEO of the Lassiter Grille Group. Can theirs be a match made in heaven, or are Jenna's scars from the past too much for her to deal with? And how will she cope when the fact they have created a new life together becomes public knowledge?

It's always a delight to be invited to participate in a Desire continuity and to work with my fellow authors on our series of linked stories. The setting for my book, Cheyenne, Wyoming, has certainly whet my appetite for more travel and my desire to learn more of this beautiful state beyond what I was able to glean from photos and articles. I hope you will enjoy reading Dylan and Jenna's story and fall in love along with them as they find their path to their own forever family and happiness.

Happy reading!

Yvonne Lindsay

EXPECTING
THE CEO'S CHILD

—

YVONNE LINDSAY

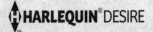

Special thanks and acknowledgment are given to Yvonne Lindsay for her contribution to the Dynasties: The Lassiters miniseries.

Recycling programs
for this product may
not exist in your area.

ISBN-13: 978-0-373-73319-4

EXPECTING THE CEO'S CHILD

Copyright © 2014 by Harlequin Books S.A.

Printed in U.S.A.

www.Harlequin.com

Books by Yvonne Lindsay

Harlequin Desire

Bought: His Temporary Fiancée #2078
The Pregnancy Contract #2117
ΩThe Wayward Son #2141
ΩA Forbidden Affair #2147
A Silken Seduction #2180
A Father's Secret #2187
ΩOne Secret Night #2217
Something About the Boss... #2252
ΩThe High Price of Secrets #2272
ΩWanting What She Can't Have #2297
Expecting the CEO's Child #2306

Silhouette Desire

*The CEO's Contract Bride #1776
*The Boss's Christmas Seduction #1758
*The Tycoon's Hidden Heir #1788
Rossellini's Revenge Affair #1811
Tycoon's Valentine Vendetta #1854
Jealousy & A Jewelled Proposition #1873
Claiming His Runaway Bride #1890
ΔConvenient Marriage, Inconvenient Husband #1923
ΔSecret Baby, Public Affair #1930
ΔPretend Mistress, Bona Fide Boss #1937
Defiant Mistress, Ruthless Millionaire #1986
^Honor-Bound Groom #2029
^Stand-In Bride's Seduction #2038
^For the Sake of the Secret Child #2044

*New Zealand Knights
ΔRogue Diamonds
^Wed at Any Price
ΩThe Master Vintners

Other titles by this author available in ebook format.

YVONNE LINDSAY

New Zealand born, to Dutch immigrant parents, Yvonne Lindsay became an avid romance reader at the age of thirteen. Now, married to her "blind date" and with two fabulous children, she remains a firm believer in the power of romance. Yvonne feels privileged to be able to bring to her readers the stories of her heart. In her spare time, when not writing, she can be found with her nose firmly in a book, reliving the power of love in all walks of life. She can be contacted via her website, www.yvonnelindsay.com.

To my dear friend Rose-Marie, who has known me since we were both teenagers—thank you for always being my friend and an especial thank you for calling florists in Wyoming for me! :) I owe you, Smithy!

One

Jenna puzzled over the complex wreath design a family had requested for their grandmother's funeral the coming Wednesday. She just about had it nailed; all she needed to confirm with the wholesale suppliers was that she'd be able to get the right shade of lilacs that had been the grandmother's favorite.

The sound of the door buzzer alerted her to a customer out front. She listened to see if her new Saturday part-time assistant would attend to the client, but the subsequent ding of the counter bell told her that Millie was likely in the cool room out back, or, unfortunately more likely, outside on the phone to her boyfriend again.

Making a mental note to discuss with the girl the importance of actually *working* during work hours, Jenna pushed herself up from her desk, pasted a smile on her face and walked out into the showroom. Only to feel the smile freeze in place as she recognized Dylan Lassiter, in all his decadent glory, standing with his back to her, his attention apparently captured by the ready-made bouquets she kept in the refrigerated unit along one wall.

Her reaction was instantaneous; heat, desire and shock flooded her in turn. The last time she'd seen him had been in the coat closet where they'd impulsively sought refuge—to release the sexual energy that had ignited so dangerously and suddenly between them. They'd struck sparks off one another so bright and so fierce it had almost been a relief when he'd returned to his base in Los Angeles. Almost.

Jenna fought the urge to place a hand protectively across her belly—to hide the evidence of that uncharacteristic and spontaneous act. She'd known from the day her pregnancy was confirmed that she'd have to tell him at some stage. She hadn't planned for it to be right now. At first she'd been a little piqued that he'd made no effort to contact her since that one incredible encounter. She had half understood he'd been too busy to call her in the aftermath of his father's sudden death during Dylan's sister's wedding rehearsal dinner. But afterward? When everything had begun to settle down again?

She gave herself a mental shake. No, she'd successfully convinced herself that she didn't need or want the complication of a relationship. Especially not now and especially not with someone as high profile as Dylan Lassiter. Not after all the years of work she'd put into rebuilding her reputation. She'd made a conscious choice to put off contacting him, too, and despite the slight wound to her feminine ego that he'd obviously done the same, she would just have to get over it because she sure as heck had plenty else to keep her mind occupied now.

"Can I help you?" she said, feigning a lack of recognition right up until the moment he turned around and impaled her with those cerulean-blue eyes of his.

Air fled from her lungs and her throat closed up. A perfectly tailored blue-gray suit emphasized the width of his shoulders, while his white shirt and pale blue tie emphasized the California tan that warmed his skin. Her mouth dried. It was a crime against nature that any man could look so beautiful and so masculine at the same time.

A hank of softly curling hair fell across his high forehead, making her hand itch to smooth it back, then trace the stubbled line of his jaw. She clenched her fingers into a tight fist, embedding her nails in her palms as she reminded herself exactly where such an action would inevitably lead.

He was like a drug to her. An instant high that, once taken, created a craving like no other. She'd spent the past two and a half months in a state of disbelief at her actions. She, who'd strived to be so careful—to keep her nose clean and to fly under the radar—was now carrying the child of a man she'd met the day it was conceived. A man she'd barely known, yet knew so much about. Certainly enough not to have succumbed the way she had.

It had literally been a one-night *stand,* she reminded herself cynically. The coat closet hadn't allowed for anything else. But as close as the confines had been, her body still remembered every second of how he'd made her feel—and it reacted in kind again.

"Jenna," Dylan said with a slow nod of his head, his gaze not moving from her face for so much as a second.

"Dylan," she replied, taking a deep breath and feigning surprise. "What brings you back to Cheyenne?"

The instant she said the words she silently groaned. The opening. Of course he was here for that. The local chamber of commerce—heck, the whole town—was abuzz with the news. She'd tried to ignore anything Lassiter-related for weeks now, but there was no ignoring the man in front of her.

The father of her unborn child.

A noise from the back of the store made both of them

turn around. Oh, thank God. Millie had finally deigned to show up and do her job.

"Ah," Jenna said, fighting to hide her relief. "Here's Millie. She'll be able to assist you with any requirements you might have. Millie, this is Mr. Lassiter, he's opening the Lassiter Grill in town. Please make sure you give him our best service."

She sent Dylan a distracted smile and turned to go, only to feel him snag her wrist with warm strong fingers. Fingers that had done unmentionably wicked things to her and whose touch now sent a spiral of need to clench deep inside her.

"Not so fast," Dylan said, spinning her gently back to face him again. "As capable as I'm sure Millie is," he continued, flashing a smile that had the impressionable teen virtually melting on the spot, "I'd prefer to deal with you directly."

"I'm sure you would," Jenna answered as quellingly as she could. "But Millie is available to help you with your inquiry. I am not."

Her heart rate skipped up a beat as a hint of annoyance dulled his eyes.

"Scared, Jenna?"

His low tones were laced with challenge. Jenna stiffened her spine.

"Not at all, just very busy."

"Not too busy, I'm sure, to catch up with an old *friend*."

Hot color stained her cheeks. They weren't anything near approaching friends. She barely knew him any better now than she had the day they'd met—the day they were so drawn to one another that flirtation had turned to touching, and touching had turned to impassioned, frenzied lovemaking in the nearest available private space.

A butterfly whisper of movement rippled across her lower belly, shocking her into gasping aloud. Of course— the moment she'd been awaiting for weeks, her baby's first perceptible motion, would have to happen with its father standing right here in front of her.

Dylan's fingers tightened on her wrist. "Are you okay?"

"I'm fine," she said hurriedly. "Just very busy."

"Then I'll only take a few minutes of your time." He gave her a searching look. "Your office?"

Her body wilted in defeat. "Through here."

He released her wrist and she felt the cool air of the showroom swirl around her sensitized skin, as if her body instantly mourned the loss of contact, his touch. She found herself rubbing at the spot where he'd held her, as if she could somehow rub away the invisible imprint he'd left upon her.

Stop being ridiculous, she growled silently. *He was nothing to you before, aside from an out of character dalliance, and he's nothing to you now.* Logically she knew she couldn't avoid him forever. Despite the fact he was based in L.A., with the new restaurant opening here in town they were bound to cross paths again sometime. It might as well be now.

The tiny fluttering sensation rippled through her belly again, reminding her that there was a great deal more to consider than just her own feelings about seeing Dylan Lassiter. Thankfully, he hadn't noticed that her petite frame carried a new softness about it now. That her figure, rather than being taut and flat, was gently rounded as the baby's presence had suddenly become more visible at thirteen weeks.

She hadn't shared news of her pregnancy with anyone yet, and had no plans to start right now. Instead, she'd sought to hide it by changing from her usual style of figure-hugging attire to longer, more flowing lines.

As they entered the tiny office she used for administration, she gestured to the chair opposite her desk and sank, gratefully, into her own on the other side. Instead of taking the seat offered to him, Dylan sat on the edge of her desk. She couldn't help but notice the way the fine wool of his trousers skimmed his long powerful thighs, or how the fabric now stretched across his groin.

Her mouth suddenly felt parched and she turned to reach for the water jug and glasses that she kept on a credenza behind her desk.

"Water?" she offered with a croak.

"No, I'm fine, thank you."

She hastily splashed a measure of clear liquid into a glass for herself and lifted it to her lips, relishing the cooling and hydrating sensation as the drink slid over her tongue. After putting the glass down on the desk, she pulled a pad toward her and picked up a pen.

"So," she said, looking up at him. "What is it you want?"

He reached out and took the pen from her hand, laying it very deliberately down on the notepad. "I thought we could talk. You know, reminisce about old times."

Heat pooled at the apex of her thighs and she pushed her chair back from her desk. Anything to increase the distance between them.

"Look, you said a few minutes, and frankly, that's all I had. Your time's up. If there's nothing business related you need to discuss…?" She hesitated a moment, her temper snapping now at the humor reflected in his eyes. "Then you'll have to excuse me so I can attend to my work."

Dylan's sinfully sensuous lips curved into a half smile.

"You're different, Jenna. I can't quite put my finger on it, but I'll figure it out."

She fought back a groan. The man was all about detail. She knew that intimately. If she didn't get him out of here soon he was bound to notice exactly what it was that was different about her. She wasn't ready for that, not right now, anyway. She needed more time.

Before she could respond, he continued, "I want you to do the flowers for the opening. Wildflowers, grasses, rustic—that kind of thing. Can you do it?"

"I'll get my staff on to preparing some samples for you on Monday. I take it you'll be around?"

His smile widened. "Oh, yes, I'll be around. And your staff won't be handling this for me. You will."

"My staff are well trained and efficient—"

"But they're not you—and I *want* you."

His words hung in the air between them. She could feel them as if he'd actually reached out and touched her.

"You can't have me," she whispered.

"Can't I? Hmm, that's a darn shame," he said. "Because then I'd have to take my business elsewhere."

His words, so gently spoken, sent a spear of ice straight through her. It would take only a day for the news that she'd turned his business away to get through town. Less than that again before more people would follow his cue and take their business to other florists, as well. She'd fought long and hard to get a reputation as the leading florist in town and she wasn't going to lose it just like that.

She bit the inside of her cheek as she swiftly considered her options. Well, option. She really had no other choice but to take his business. Refusing it, with the associated fallout when word got around that she'd turned down a Lassiter—well, it didn't bear thinking about. However, the benefits would roll in pretty quickly when it was known that she'd done the flowers for the opening. There was nothing some of the better-heeled members of Cheyenne society loved more than following a trend set by the Lassiter family.

"I may be able to carve out a little time," she hedged, not wanting him to see how easily he'd forced her to capitulate. "Do you have particular designs in mind?"

"Tell you what. Why don't we discuss this further over dinner tonight."

"I'm sorry, I have plans for tonight." Plans that included a long soak with her feet in a tub filled with warm water and Epsom salts, followed by a home pedicure while she could still bend down and reach her toes. "Perhaps you could give me your contact number for while you're here. I'll call you when I'm free."

He gave her a narrow-eyed glance, then lazily got to his feet, reached into his back pocket for his wallet and slid out a card. She went to take it, but he didn't immediately let it go. Instead, he tugged it closer to his body, thereby tugging her a little closer, too.

"You'll call me?"

"Of course. We're closed tomorrow, but I'll check my schedule on Monday and call you then."

"I'll look forward to it," he said with a lazy wink and released the card.

She followed him from the office into the showroom. Even though she'd worked here since she was a teenager, she was still attuned to the sweet, luscious fragrance of the blooms she had on display. The various layers of scent filled the air with a strong feminine presence. A complete contrast to the powerful masculinity that was Dylan Lassiter.

Jenna held the front door to the store open for him.

"Thanks for stopping by," she said as he stepped past her and onto the sidewalk.

Just as he did, a large delivery truck passed on the street. The subsequent whoosh of warm air hit her full on, the gust plastering her short-sleeved tunic against her body. Dylan didn't miss a trick. His eyes drifted over the new fullness of her breasts, then lower, to where her waist had thickened, and to the gentle roundness of her tummy. He stared at her for what felt like an aeon before his eyes flicked upward to her face.

What she saw reflected back at her had the ability to nail her feet to the ground, right where she stood. She'd read about his convivial side, his laissez-faire attitude to life and his ability to continually land on his feet even as he eschewed traditional choices. Conversely, it was widely known that he was a perfectionist in the kitchen, which took a keen mind and grim determination.

The expression that he presented to her belonged to a different man entirely. This was the face of the CEO of the Lassiter Grill Corporation, not the playboy, not the one-time lover. No, this was the face of a man who had a question and, she thought with a shiver, would do whatever it took to get his answer.

"Looks like we have a bit more than just flowers to discuss. I think we'd best be having that dinner mighty soon, don't you?"

He turned on the heel of his hand-tooled boot and strode toward a dark SUV parked a few spaces down the street. She couldn't help but watch the lithe way his body moved. Jenna closed her eyes for a second but still his image burned there as if imprinted on her retinas. And she knew, without a shadow of a doubt, that her time for keeping this baby a secret had well and truly passed.

Two

Dylan swung his SUV into the traffic and fought to control the anger that roiled inside him like a building head of thunderclouds.

She was pregnant. No wonder she'd been as skittish as one of Sage's newborn foals when he'd arrived. He was probably the last person on earth she either expected, or wanted, to see.

His baby? The timing would be about right—unless she was the type of woman who indulged in casual assignations with just about any man she met. The thought made her stomach pitch uneasily. He needed to know for sure if their encounter had resulted in pregnancy. God, pregnancy. A kid of his own. And with her.

It wasn't hard to recall how his eye had been drawn to her that cool March Friday. He'd wanted her, right there, right then.

He remembered his first sight of her as she flitted about like some exotic bird, her attention solely on the flower arrangements she'd designed for his sister, Angelica's, wedding rehearsal dinner—a dinner that had ended before it began when his adoptive father, J.D., had collapsed with a fatal heart attack—for a wedding that had been called off, permanently now it seemed.

The building had been full of people doing what they did best, but Jenna stood out among them all in her jewel bright colors. An effervescent energy simply vibrated off her. Their initial banter had been fun and she'd given as good as she got. But the real craziness had started the moment he caught her hand in his and pulled her into an alcove where he kissed her, so he could see for himself if she tasted as intoxicating as he'd imagined.

She'd spun out of his arms the instant he'd loosened his hold on her but the imprint of her slight frame against his body had stayed with him through the course of the next hour, until he'd known that one kiss was definitely not enough. Satisfied the catering team in the kitchen knew what they were doing, he'd hunted Jenna down as she'd applied the finishing touches to the floral design she'd created for the entrance to the Cheyenne Depot—a historic railroad station that had been converted into a popular reception hall. Hunted her down and entrapped her in his arms for what he'd planned to be just one more kiss.

One more kiss had turned into a frenzy of need and they'd found their way into the coat closet at the front of the building. In its dark recesses, they'd discovered just what level of delight they could bring each other to.

He'd never been the kind of guy who waited for anything to come to him. No, he always went out and got it. And he'd certainly gone out and gotten her—both of them swept along on a tide of attraction that still left him breathless whenever he thought about it. He'd had casual encounters before, but this had been so very different. But then his father had died and his world had changed.

By the time the formalities here in Cheyenne had been taken care of, he'd had to race back to L.A. to continue his duties as CEO of the Lassiter Grill Corporation. Hassling Angelica for the contact details of the florist she'd used for that night—a night from which repercussions continued to cause his sister pain—had seemed a cruel and unnecessary thing to do. Besides, he'd had enough on his plate with work. Now, it seemed, he had a great deal more.

His inattention to the road forced him to jam on his brakes when the traffic ahead slowed suddenly. He swore softly. Two hours. He'd give her two hours to call him about dinner—max. If she hadn't phoned by then, he'd sure as heck be calling her.

In the end it was fifty-eight minutes exactly before his cell phone began vibrating in his pocket. He took it out, a smile curving his lips as he saw the name of her store come up on the screen.

"I was thinking we could make it tonight," he said without preamble. "My place, seven o'clock."

"Y-your place?"

He rattled off the address. "You know where it is?"

"Sure. I'll find it," she answered, her voice a little breathless.

"Maybe I ought to pick you up. Don't want you changing your mind at the last minute."

"I won't, I promise. I'll see you at seven."

She hung up before he could say another thing. His mouth firmed into a grim line as he slid his phone back into his pocket. It was a rare thing indeed to find a woman of so few words. Even when they'd first met they'd been bigger on action than conversation.

That was certainly going to change. He had a list of questions as long as his arm and he wasn't letting her go until she'd answered every last one.

One thing was certain. If she was carrying his child, he was going to be a part of that baby's life. Losing his own parents when he was young, then being raised by his aunt Ellie and her husband, J. D. Lassiter, Dylan knew just how important family was. He'd been too young to remember his mom and dad properly, too young to mourn more than the sense of security he'd taken for granted from birth. After his parents died, however, that all changed, until Aunt Ellie and J.D. stepped in and ensured that he, his brother, Sage, and sister, Angelica, never wanted for a thing. Even after Ellie Lassiter passed away, her sister-in-law, Marlene, had become a surrogate mom to them. It had been family that had gotten them through.

Now, with J.D. gone, too, the whole concept of family was even more important to him than ever. His brother thought he was nuts putting so much store by it. At constant loggerheads with J.D. and determined to make his own place in the world, Sage had always insisted that the only family he needed was Dylan. As close as they were, Dylan had always wanted more. And, if Jenna Montgomery's baby was his, it looked like he might be getting it.

Jenna reluctantly got ready to go out to Dylan's place. He was a complication she would rather ignore right now, but clearly, he wasn't about to let that happen. She quickly showered, then took her time rubbing scented moisturizer into her skin. So what if she had just shaved her legs—they needed it. She certainly hadn't done it for *his* benefit.

Nor had she applied the makeup she barely ever wore anymore for him, either. She was doing this all for herself. Pure and simple. If it made her feel good, feel stronger, then she was doing it. The same principle applied to the clothes she'd chosen to wear tonight. The royal purple stretch lace dress flattered her figure, even with the additional curves that now showed. It empowered her, as did the black spike-heeled pumps she teetered on.

She paused for a moment to assess herself in the mirror. Too much? Her eyes scanned from her dark brown hair, worn loose and flat-ironed dead straight, to her shiny patent leather shoes. She swiveled sideways. This was a total contrast to the kind of thing she'd worn in recent weeks. And, yes, it was definitely too much—which was why she wasn't going to change a thing.

She grabbed her purse from the bed and told herself she was not nervous about this meeting. That's all it was. A meeting. She'd tell Dylan what she'd been planning to tell him all along, and that would be that.

She wouldn't be swayed by the depth of his blue eyes, or the careless fall of his hair, which always looked as if he'd just tumbled from bed. She knew he was handsome; she'd fallen prey to that so easily. She also knew he was successful and intelligent and had a charm that could melt a polar ice cap. But she'd be immune to all that now, too. At least she hoped she would be.

She'd had weeks to think about this. Weeks in which to decide that while Dylan should know about his baby, she was most definitely bringing it up on her own. She knew full well what not to do when raising a child. Her own parents had been the prime example of that. No, her baby would want for nothing. He or she would grow up secure in the knowledge of Jenna's love and protection.

A man like Dylan Lassiter, with his cavalier lifestyle, a girl for every day of the week, every week of the year, not to mention his celebrity status, which ensured he traveled constantly, did not fit into the picture at all. She'd taken a walk on that wild side of his and yes, she had enjoyed every precious second. But life, real life, had to be lived in a far more stable and measured way. She owned her own home and had a business that was doing well…. With a few economies she could and would do this all on her own.

With those thoughts to arm her, she locked up and

walked out to her car. Checking the map one more time, she headed north to the address he'd given her, on the outskirts of town.

Doubts began to assail Jenna as she pulled in between the massive gated pillars, each adorned with a wrought-iron, stylized *L,* at the entrance to the driveway. The drive itself had to be several football fields long. She knew the family was wealthy, but seriously, who did this? Who kept a property this immense when they spent only about two months of every year living here? The Lassiters, that's who. It was a stark and somewhat intimidating reminder of the differences between herself and Dylan, and it struck a nervous chime deep inside her.

What if he used his money and his position to make things difficult for her? She had no idea what he was really like, although she remembered, without the slightest hesitation, how he'd felt and how he'd tasted. He was forbidden fruit. The kind of man every woman, no matter her age, turned her head to watch go past. The kind of man every woman deserved to savor—as Jenna had—at least once in her lifetime. But he wasn't a forever kind of guy. She'd been thankful he hadn't contacted her after their…their…*tryst,* she reminded herself again. She definitely wasn't looking for the roller coaster ride or the intrusive media publicity a relationship with him would offer.

Almost everything she knew about Dylan Lassiter she'd gleaned from social media and word of mouth around town—of which there was plenty. He'd basically gone wherever whim had taken him, spurning the opportunities and advantages afforded him by his adoptive father, and refusing to go into the family business or even attend college. Jenna sighed. What would it have been like, she wondered, to be able to be so carefree? She knew he'd traveled widely, eventually training in Europe as a chef and then coming back to L.A. and building a solid name for his skills, together with a certain celebrity notoriety at the same time. His life, to her, just seemed so...*indulgent.*

Her upbringing had been as different from Dylan's as a bridal bouquet was from a sizzling steak platter. And from her perspective, while there was plenty about Dylan Lassiter to recommend him to anyone who liked to run fast and loose, there was very little to recommend him as father material.

That said, this baby was *their* creation. Dylan had rights—and she had no plans to stand in the way of those. But she also wanted her child to grow up secure, in one place, with a stable and loving parent. Not used in a tug-of-war between parents, as she had been. Not dragged from pillar to post as her father moved from country to country, then state to state in pursuit of some unattainable happily-ever-after. And certainly not implicated by her father's fraudulent schemes or left abandoned at the age of fifteen because her sole surviving parent was doing time in jail.

No, Jenna's baby was going to have everything she hadn't.

She gently applied the brake and her car came to a stop outside the impressive portico. She rested a hand on the slight mound of her belly, determined not to be totally overwhelmed by the obvious wealth on display before her. This baby had rights, too, and yes, he or she was entitled to be a part of what stood before Jenna. But right now she was the baby's only advocate, and she knew what was best for him or her. And she'd fight to her very last breath to ensure her child got exactly that.

She grabbed her bag and got out of the car. The front

door opened as she walked toward it, and Dylan stood on the threshold. Jenna's heart did that little double skip, just as it had the very first time she saw him. It was hard to remain objective when the man stood before her. He'd tamed his hair slightly, giving him a more refined look, and he'd changed his suit for a pale blue cotton shirt that made his eyes seem even bluer than before.

"You found the place okay?" he asked unnecessarily as she ascended the wide steps.

"Hard to miss it, don't you think?" she replied, not even bothering to keep the note of acerbity from her tone.

She didn't want him to think even for a minute that he had the upper hand in this meeting. He inclined his head slightly, as if acknowledging she'd scored a valid point.

"Come on in," he invited, opening the door wide. "You must be ready to put your feet up after working all day. Can I get you something to drink?"

"Just mineral water, if you have it, thanks."

She hadn't drunk alcohol since she'd known she might be pregnant. In fact, there were a lot of things she didn't eat or drink as a result of the changes happening deep inside her body.

"Sure, take a seat," he said, gesturing to the large and comfortable-looking furniture that dominated the living room off the main entrance. "I'll be right back."

He was as good as his word. She'd barely settled herself against the butter-soft leather of a sofa big enough to sleep on before he was back with two drinks. An ice-cold beer for himself and a tall glass of sparkling water for her.

"Thank you," she said stiffly, taking the glass from his hand and studiously avoiding making eye contact.

But she couldn't avoid the slight brush of fingers, nor could she ignore the zing of awareness that speared through her at that faint touch. She rapidly lifted the glass to her lips to mask her reaction. The bubbles leaping from the water's surface tickled her nose, further irritating her. She swallowed carefully and put the glass on the coaster on the table in front of her.

Dylan sprawled in the seat opposite, his large, rangy frame filling the chair. His gaze never left her face and an increasingly uncomfortable silence stretched out between them. Jenna cleared her throat nervously. Obviously, she was going to have to start this conversation.

"I—I wanted to say how sorry I was about your father's passing."

"Thank you."

"He was much respected and I'm sure you must miss him very much," she persisted.

"I do," Dylan acknowledged, then took a long draw of his beer.

Damn him, he wasn't making this easy for her. But then again, what had she expected?

"He'd have been proud of the new restaurant opening here in town," she continued valiantly.

"That he would."

"And you? You must be pleased with everything being on time."

"I am."

A muscle tugged at the edge of his mouth, pulling his lips into a half smile that was as cynical as it was appealing. Jenna suddenly had the overwhelming sense that she shouldn't have come here. That perhaps she should have waited a day or two before calling him. Hard on its heels came the contradictory but certain knowledge that she definitely should have been in touch with him long before now.

Was this how a mouse felt, she wondered, just before a cat pounced? Did it feel helpless, confused and frightened, with nowhere to look but straight into a maw of dread?

She watched, mesmerized, as Dylan leaned forward and carefully put his beer on the table. He rested his elbows on his knees, those sinfully dexterous hands of his loosely clasped between them. Warmth unfurled from her core like a slowly opening bud, and she forced her eyes to lift upward, to meet the challenge in his.

She fought to suppress a shudder when she saw the determination that reflected back at her. She reached for her water and took another sip, shocked to discover that her hand shook ever so slightly. She dug deep for the last ounce of courage she possessed. Since he was determined to make this so awkward, she'd find some inane way to carry the conversation even if it killed her.

"Thank you for asking me to dinner tonight. It's not every day I'm catered to by a European-trained celebrity chef."

She was surprised to hear Dylan sigh, as if he was disappointed in something. In her?

"Jenna, stop dancing around the issue and cut to the chase. Are you pregnant with my baby?"

Three

Dylan cursed inwardly. He'd been determined to be charming. He could do charming with his eyes closed and both hands behind his back. So why, then, had he so ham-fistedly screwed up what he'd planned to be a relaxing evening of fact-finding with a woman he'd been fiercely attracted to from the second he'd first laid eyes on her?

It was too late now. The words were out and he couldn't drag them back no matter how much he wanted to. He huffed out a breath of frustration. Jenna looked about as stunned by his question as he was at actually blurting it out that way. Damage control. He desperately needed to go into damage control mode, but try as he might, he couldn't think of the words to say. What he wanted was the answer. An answer that only Jenna Montgomery could provide.

Beneath his gaze she appeared to shrink a little into the voluminous furniture. She was already a dainty thing— her small body perfectly formed—but right now she was dwarfed by her surroundings and, no doubt, daunted by the conversation they were about to have.

Dylan knew he should try and put her at ease, but the second she'd alighted from her car he had felt the shields she'd erected between them. It had aroused a side of him he hadn't displayed in years, made him deliberately uncooperative as she'd tried to observe the niceties of polite conversation. It had driven him to ask the question that had been plaguing him since that gust of wind off the road had revealed changes in her slender form that were too obvious to someone who knew that form as intimately, even if fleetingly, as he had.

"Well?" he prompted.

"Yes," she said in a strangled whisper.

Dylan didn't know what to say. Inside he felt as if he'd just scored a touchdown at the Super Bowl, but he also had this weird feeling of detachment, as if he was looking in on some other guy's life. As if what she'd just said wasn't real—didn't involve him. But he was involved, very much so. Or at least he *would* be, whether she liked it or not.

"Were you going to tell me sometime, or did you just hope that I'd never know?"

As much as he fought to keep the hard note of anger from his voice, he could feel it lacing every word. It left a bitter taste in his mouth and he struggled to pull himself under control. He didn't want to antagonize her or scare her away, and it wasn't as if he'd made an effort to get in touch with her again before today. This was way too important, and at the crux of it all an innocent child's future depended on the outcome of tonight.

"I meant to tell you, and I was going to—in my own time. I've been busy and I had a bit of a struggle coming to terms with it myself. Getting my head around how I'm going to cope."

Jenna's voice shook, but even though she was upset, he sensed the shields she'd erected earlier growing even thicker, her defense even stronger.

"And you didn't think I should have known about this earlier?"

"What difference would it have made?"

Her words shocked him. What difference? Did she think that knowing he was going to be a father made no discernible difference to his life, to how he felt about *everything?* Hell, he'd lost his own father only a couple months ago. Didn't she think he at least deserved a light in the darkness of mourning? Something to get him through the responsibility of having to get up every day and keep putting one foot in front of the other, all because so many other people depended on him to not only do exactly that, but to do it brilliantly—even when he wanted to wallow in grief?

"Trust me." He fought to keep his tone even. "It would have made a difference. When did you know?"

"About three weeks after we—" Her voice broke off and she appeared to gather up her courage before she spoke again. "I began to suspect I might be pregnant, and waited another week before going to my doctor."

Dylan sucked in a breath between his teeth. So, by his reckoning, she'd had confirmation that their encounter had resulted in conception for plenty of time. She could have shared the news—no matter how busy she was.

Damn it, he'd used a condom; they should have been safe. But nothing was 100 percent effective, except maybe abstinence. And there was one thing that was guaranteed, when it came to Jenna: abstinence was the last thing on Dylan's mind.

Even now, as quietly irate as he was right this second, she still had a power over him. His skin felt too tight for his body, as if he was itching to burst out and lose himself in her. His flesh stirred to life even as the idea took flight. Desire uncoiled from the pit of his belly and sent snaking tendrils in a heated path throughout him.

No one had had that power over him before. Ever.

Yet this diminutive woman had once driven him to a sexual frenzy that had tipped over into sheer madness. She still could.

A ringing sound penetrated Dylan's consciousness, a much needed reminder of the here and now and the fact that Jenna sat opposite him, quite a different woman from the one he'd so quickly but thoroughly made love to two and a half months ago.

"I'll be right back," he said, surreptitiously adjusting himself as he rose from the seat. "I need to check on something in the kitchen."

After a quick examination of the beef bourguignonne simmering on the stovetop, and checking that the rice in the cooker was fluffy and ready, he grunted with satisfaction. They would continue this discussion at the table, where, hopefully, he'd find his manners again and stand a better chance of hiding the effect she had on him.

He returned to the living room and painted a smile on his face.

"Dinner's ready. Would you like to come through to the kitchen? I thought we could eat in there, if you're comfortable with that."

"Since I usually eat standing up at the store or off a tray on my lap when I'm home, just sitting at a table sounds lovely."

She stood and smoothed her clothes, her hand lingering on the tiny bump that revealed a child of his now existed. It hit Dylan like a fist to the chest. His child. Someone of his blood. Everything else in his life right now faded into the background as that knowledge took precedence. Now there was another generation to think about, to protect and to teach.

The thought filled him with a new sense of purpose, of hope. The past five years had been challenging, the past couple of months even more so. But this baby was a new beginning. A reason for Dylan to ground himself in what was good, and to put some much needed balance back in his life, balance that was sadly lacking. This baby, his son or daughter, was a lifeline out of a spiral of work and hard play that had threatened to consume him. One way or another he would be a part of his child's world—every single day if he could, although that would take some engineering with him based in L.A. and Jenna here in Cheyenne. Whatever the logistics, he was prepared to work this situation out. He just needed to be certain that Jenna felt the same way.

She crossed the room to where he stood, and he put his hand at the small of her back and guided her through to the kitchen. He felt her stiffen slightly beneath his touch, and heard her breath hitch just a little. Knowing she wasn't as unaffected by him as she pretended went a long way toward making him feel better about the semi-erection he was constantly battling to keep in control.

He seated her at the square wooden table in the kitchen and gestured to the vase containing a handful of wild-flowers he'd found on his four-acre property when he'd gone to walk off some steam this afternoon.

"They could probably have done with your touch," he said as he turned to the oven to take warmed plates out and lay them on the table.

"They look fine just the way they are," Jenna commented.

But as if she couldn't resist, he saw her reach out and tweak a few stems. Before he knew it, the bouquet looked a hundred times better.

"How do you do that?" he asked, bringing the Dutch oven filled with the deliciously fragrant beef across from the stove.

"Do what?"

"Make a jumble of weeds look so good."

She shrugged. "It's a knack I picked up, I guess."

"What made you decide to work with flowers?"

"I didn't, really." She sighed. "They kind of picked me."

"Not a family business, then?" he probed, curious to discover just how she had ended up under Mrs. Connell's roof.

Jenna gave a rueful laugh. "No, not a family business at all, although once I started working at the store it felt like home to me."

There was a wistful note in her voice, one he wanted to explore further, but found himself reluctant to. There was time enough to find out all her secrets, he told himself.

He spooned rice from the cooker onto the warmed plates, and put them on the table.

"This looks great," Jenna commented, leaning forward to inhale deeply. "And smells even better. To be honest, I think your skills with food far outweigh mine with flowers. I can barely reheat a TV dinner without burning something."

Dylan feigned horror. "Wash your mouth out. TV dinners? You're going to have to do much better than that for the baby."

He reached for a ladle and spooned a generous portion of the beef onto her plate before serving himself. When she didn't immediately pick up her fork, he sat back and looked at her. Her lips had firmed into a mutinous line and there was a frown of annoyance on her forehead.

"What did I say?"

"I didn't come here to be told what to do. Maybe it's better if I go."

She pushed back her chair a little, but before she could go any farther he reached out and grabbed her hand.

"Okay, truce. I will try not to tell you what to eat, but you have to admit, for me it comes with the territory. It's what I do. It's in my nature to want to feed people well."

It was also in his nature to want to lift her from her chair, march her to the nearest accommodatingly soft surface and relive some of the passion they'd shared. She looked down at where his fingers were curled around her wrist, and he slowly eased his grip and let her go.

"As long as we're clear on that," she muttered, scooting her chair closer to the table again and lifting her fork.

She scooped up a mouthful and brought it to her lips. His brain ceased to function as she closed her eyes and moaned in pleasure. Other body parts had no such difficulty.

"That's so good," she said, opening her eyes again.

For a second Dylan allowed himself to be lost in their chocolate-brown depths. Just a second. Then he forced himself to look away and apply himself to his own meal.

"Thanks, I aim to please," he said with a nonchalance he was far from feeling.

It didn't seem to matter what he did or what he said, or even how she reacted to any of it—he was drawn to her on a level he'd never experienced before. Sure, that could play to his advantage, but he had the sneaking suspicion that Jenna Montgomery was a great deal more hard-headed than her feminine presence at his table suggested.

"Home grown?" she asked, spearing some beef and popping it into her mouth.

For a second he was distracted by her lips closing around the fork, then the enticing half smile they curved into as she tasted and chewed.

"Yeah, from the Big Blue. Nothing but the best."

"Your cousin runs it, doesn't he? Chance Lassiter?"

"And very well, too. It's in his blood."

And therein lay the rub. While he and Sage had been raised Lassiters, they weren't Lassiter by birth. Not like Chance, not like their sister, Angelica. It was one of the reasons why this baby meant so much more to Dylan than he had ever imagined. This child was a part of his legacy, his mark on the world. It was all very well gaining fame and fortune for doing something you excelled at and loved, but raising a child and setting him or her on a path for life—nothing compared to that.

"Have you thought about what you're going to do when the baby is born?" he asked, deliberately changing the subject.

"Do?"

"About work."

"I'll manage. I figure that in the early stages I should be able to keep the baby at work with me."

He nodded, turning the idea over in his mind. "Yes, sure—initially. I think that would be a good idea."

"I'm sorry?"

He looked at her in puzzlement. But his confusion didn't last long.

"What you think should matter to me, why, exactly?"

He let his fork clatter onto his plate. "Well, it is my baby, too. I have some say in what happens to him or her."

Even though he'd tried to keep his voice neutral, some of his frustration must have leaked through.

"Dylan, as far as I'm concerned, while you have rights to be a part of this baby's life, it doesn't mean you have a say in how I bring it up."

"Oh? And how do you see that working? Just let me jet in every now and then, have a visit and then jet out again?"

"Pretty much. After all, you live most of the time in L.A., or wherever else in the world you're flying off to—not here where the baby and I will be. Obviously, I won't stand in your way when you want to see him or her, though, as long as it's clear I'm the one raising the child."

That was not how things were going to happen. Dylan's hands curled into fists on the table and took in a deep, steadying breath. "That's good of you," he said, as evenly as he could. "Although I have another suggestion, one that I find far more palatable, and which will be better for all of us."

She looked at him in surprise. "Oh? What's that?"

"That we get married and raise the baby together."

To his chagrin she laughed. Not just laughed but snorted and snuffled with it as if she couldn't contain her mirth.

"It's not so impossible to think of, is it?" he demanded.

"Impossible? It's ridiculous, Dylan. We barely know one another."

He nodded in agreement. "True. That's something easily rectified."

All humor fled from her face. "You're serious, aren't you?"

"Never more so."

"No. It would never work. Not in a million years."

"Why not? We already know we're…" he paused a moment for effect, his eyes skimming her face, her throat and lower "…compatible."

"Great sex isn't the sole basis for a compatible marriage," she protested.

"It's a start," he said, his voice deepening.

Hot color danced in her cheeks—due to anger or something else? he wondered. Something like desire, perhaps?

"Not for me it isn't. Look, can we agree to disagree on

the subject of marriage? I've already said I won't stand in your way when it comes to seeing the child. Can we leave it at that for now?"

"Sure, for now. But, Jenna, one thing you will learn about me is that I never give up. Especially not on something this important."

Four

Jenna's heart hammered a steady drumbeat in her chest. He looked deadly serious. This wasn't how she had imagined their meal together going, not at all. She certainly hadn't imagined that he'd spring an offer of marriage on her like that.

Sure, there was probably a list as long as her arm of women who would jump at the opportunity. But she wasn't like that. And she'd meant it when she'd said his life was in L.A. and not here, because it *was*. While it was true that he'd been in Wyoming more often lately, it was only because of the new Grill opening in town. Once that was up and running he'd be straight back to the West Coast. Back to his high life and being featured in the celebrity news with his beautiful women.

No, marriage to Dylan Lassiter didn't even bear thinking of, she decided as she forced herself to take another bite of the melt-in-your-mouth perfection of the meal he'd prepared. He might be spending more time in the boardroom these days, she mused, but he hadn't lost his knack in the kitchen.

Maybe it would be worth marrying him just to have meals like this every day, she thought flippantly. An image of him barefoot and in the kitchen, wearing an apron and not much else, hovered in her mind, sending a pull of longing through her.

No, get a grip on yourself, she chided silently. She'd never settled for anything less than perfection when it came to a relationship. It was why she so rarely dated. That was why her behavior with Dylan back in March was such an aberration.

Once people began to notice her pregnancy, she had no doubt there'd be a whole ton of questions asked. Uncomfortable questions. Her hard-fought-for privacy would be invaded—her reputation open for all of Cheyenne to discuss. It shouldn't bother her, but it did. She knew what it was like to be the focus of unwanted attention, and she'd worked hard to stay out of the public eye ever since.

"I'm glad you acknowledge that our child is important. I happen to agree, which is why I'm not going to rush into anything or make any decisions today," she finally stated.

"You're important, too, Jenna," he answered softly.

For a second she felt a swelling in her chest—a glimmer of something ephemeral, an intangible dream emerging on the periphery of her thoughts. Then reality intruded. She shook her head.

"Don't lie to me, Dylan. We both know that since March neither of us has made any attempt to contact or see one another, until today. In fact, if you didn't have the restaurant opening coming up, we probably wouldn't even be here right now."

"I don't know about you, but I've thought about that evening a lot."

Jenna couldn't stop the warm tingling sensation that spread from the pit of her belly at his words.

"Don't!" she blurted.

"Don't what? Don't admit that we were blisteringly good together? Tell me you haven't thought about us, about what we did—and haven't wanted to try again. Even just to see if it wasn't some kind of weird fluke."

"I—"

Her throat closed up, blocked by a swell of need so fierce it overwhelmed her. She forced herself to erase the visual image that now burned in the back of her mind. An image he'd put there without so much as a speck of effort because it was always there, always waiting to be brought out into the light and examined, relived. She squirmed on her seat, suddenly uncomfortable, aching. For him. For more.

"Fine," she muttered curtly. "We were good together, but that's no basis for a future. We are two totally different people. Our lives barely intersect."

"That's not to say that they couldn't. Don't you want to just try it?"

He looked so earnest, sitting there opposite her at the table. It would be all too easy to give in, but she'd worked too hard for too damn long to even consider giving up her hard-won freedom, not to mention her hard-earned respect from the community.

She herself had been the product of a hurried marriage, one that hadn't worked on any level and had led to hardship and unhappiness for all concerned. She would not inflict that on her baby. No matter how enticing that baby's father was. No matter how much she wanted him.

What did he know of marriage, of commitment? Their own liaison was a perfect example of the impulsive life he led. See something? Want it? Have it, then just walk away without a backward glance. She couldn't risk that he'd do that with their child, let alone her. Not now, not ever.

"No," she said firmly. "I don't. Please don't push me on this issue, Dylan."

"Okay," he acceded.

She felt her shoulders relax.

"For today," he amended.

And the tension was right back again. He cracked a smile and she was struck again by his male beauty. There was not a thing about him, physically at least, that didn't set her body on fire. As to his morals, well, that was something else entirely. But her behavior didn't reflect so well on her, either, she reminded herself.

"Don't look so serious, Jenna. We'll declare a truce for this evening, all right?"

His voice was coaxing, warm. And almost her very undoing.

"Truce, then," she agreed, and applied herself again to her meal.

It truly was too good to ignore and, much as she hated to admit it, he was right that she should be eating better. Weariness had been quite an issue for her, and while prenatal vitamins and supplements were helping, nothing really substituted for a healthy diet and plenty of rest.

"More?" Dylan asked when her plate was empty.

"I'm stuffed," she said, leaning back in her chair with a smile on her face. "That was excellent, thank you."

"Just part of the package," he said with a smile. "So, are you too stuffed to think about dessert? Can I tempt you with some raspberry and white chocolate cheesecake?"

"Tempt me? Are you kidding? Of course I want dessert."

When he took the dish from the refrigerator she almost dissolved into a puddle of delight.

"You made that, too?" she asked as he sliced a piece for her. She reached out and nabbed a white chocolate curl from off the top, laughing as he went to slap her hand away and missed.

"Not me personally this time. It's one of the desserts

we're trialing for the steak house," he said, sliding her plate toward her. "I picked it up this afternoon."

She spooned up a taste and then another.

"Good?" Dylan asked.

"Divine. Don't talk to me, you're messing with my concentration."

He laughed aloud and the sound traveled straight to her heart and gave it a fierce tug. *Oh, yeah, it was all too easy to think you could fall in love with a man like Dylan Lassiter,* she told herself. He was the whole package. Not just tall, dark and handsome, but wealthy, entertaining to be with and bloody good in bed. Well, in a coat closet, anyway. And then there was the near orgasmic cooking.

Don't go there, she warned herself. But it was too late. Arousal spread through her like a wildfire. Licking and teasing at her until she felt her breasts grow full and achy, her nipples tightening and becoming almost unbearably sensitive against the sheer fabric of her bra. She knew the very second Dylan's line of vision moved, the precise moment he became aware of her reaction.

"Remind me to feed you cheesecake more often," he said, his voice slightly choked. "I'm going to make coffee. Can I offer you some, or a cup of something else, maybe?"

"Hot tea, please," Jenna answered, fighting to get her wayward hormones back under control.

Dylan stood and turned away from the table, but not before she noticed he wasn't exactly unaffected himself. So it seemed the crazy attraction between them showed no sign of abating. What on earth was she going to do about it?

Nothing. Abso-freaking-lutely nothing at all. They'd get through the rest of this evening. They might even discuss the baby a little more. But they were not going to do a single thing about this undeniable magnetism between them. After all, look where it had led them the last time.

Dylan ground fresh coffee beans and measured them into his coffeemaker, taking his time over the task. This was getting ridiculous. Why couldn't she see just how suited they were to one another? Why wouldn't anyone want to take that further? Her physical attraction to him was painstakingly obvious. Not that he needed any help in that department, but it was a natural trigger for his own.

There was a lot to be said for being a caveman, he thought as he switched on the electric kettle and heated the water for her tea. He'd never before felt so inclined to drag a woman by her hair into his lair and keep her there—making love to her until she no longer wanted to leave. He gave himself a mental shake. No, that image was completely unacceptable. He liked his women willing. He'd never used force or coercion before and he wouldn't start now—no matter how tempting Ms. Jenna Montgomery made the idea seem. Somehow, he had to make her see that they'd be good together. Good enough for marriage and raising a kid.

He heard the scrape of her spoon on the plate as she finished her cheesecake, and he returned to the table with their hot drinks on a tray.

"Shall we take these back through to the living room?" he suggested.

"Sure."

She got up to follow him and his eyes drifted again to her belly, to where his baby lay safely nestled. It roused something feral in him. Something he'd never experienced before today. Something he knew, deep in his heart, would never go away. He knew it was possible to love another person's child—knew it from firsthand experience, from *being* that child, from being loved. For some reason, though, knowing it was his son or daughter she carried made Dylan feel as if he could give a certain superhero a decent run for his money in the leaping tall buildings department.

He also knew he'd do anything, lay down his life if necessary, to provide the best for his kid.

Jenna returned to her seat on the sofa and Dylan sat next to her, a sense of satisfaction spreading inside when she didn't scoot away from him.

"When's the baby due?" he asked, after taking a sip of his coffee.

"First week in December, all going well."

"A baby by Christmas," he mused aloud, struck by how much his life could change in a year.

"Life will be different, that's for sure."

"So what have you planned so far?"

Suddenly he needed to know everything she'd already done, and what she wanted to do for the rest of her pregnancy. This should involve him.

"Well, I've started getting a few things for the spare room in my house, you know, to turn it into a nursery. I found a bassinet at a yard sale last weekend. I'm going to reline it and get a collapsible stand. That way I'll be able to use it in my office at the store as well as at home, until the baby gets a little bigger."

Dylan suppressed the shudder that threatened to run through him at the thought that his child would have secondhand anything. Did that make him a snob? Probably. He and his brother had shared things as they grew up, and there'd been nothing wrong with that. It didn't stop him from wanting to race out to the nearest store and buy all new equipment for his child, though.

Jenna, sensitive already, obviously picked up on his thoughts. "What's wrong? You think our baby is too good for a secondhand bassinet?"

"Actually," he started, thinking he needed to tread very carefully, "I was thinking more along the lines of what I could do to help out financially."

If she was scouring yard sales, maybe she was a bit stretched when it came to money. She had the store, but also had her own home. Financing both took a lot of hard work and determination. And dollars and cents.

"I can manage, you know," she said defensively.

"The point is you don't have to *manage*," he said. "I meant what I said when I told you I'm going to be a part of this baby's life, and I don't just mean the occasional visit. I'm happy to support you both."

She looked as if she was about to bristle and reject his words, but then she slumped a little, as though a load had been lifted from her slender shoulders.

"Thank you." She sighed softly. "It won't be necessary, but I do appreciate the offer."

"Hey," he said, taking one of her hands in his and mentally comparing how small and dainty it felt in his much larger palm. It roused a fierce sense of protection inside him. One he knew would be smacked straight into next week if he showed her even an inkling of how she made him feel. "We got into this together, and that's how it's going to stay."

She looked up at him, her dark eyes awash with moisture. "Do you think we can do that? Stay friends through this?"

"Of course we can."

"It's not going to be easy."

"Nothing worthwhile ever is," he commented.

At the same time he promised himself that no matter

what, she would not be doing this on her own. And one way or another, he'd get her to change her mind about marrying him. Now that he had her back in his life, he didn't want to let her go again. There was a damn fine reason why he hadn't been able to shake her image from his thoughts every single day. Now he had every incentive to find out exactly what that reason was.

Five

By the time Jenna rose to leave, weariness pulled at every muscle in her body. She was grateful tomorrow was Sunday. A blessed day of rest, with time to weigh up everything that had happened since Dylan Lassiter had walked back into her life. Maybe she'd get to work in the garden for a while, too—she always found that restful. Or even a lazy stroll around the Cheyenne Botanic Gardens might be nice.

"It's late," she said, stifling a yawn. "I'd better get home. Thank you for tonight. I mean that."

"You're welcome," Dylan replied, getting to his feet and putting his hand at the small of her back again.

Despite her exhaustion, her body responded instantly. It would be so easy to give in. To turn toward him, press her body against his large hard frame and sink into the attraction between them. To allow him back behind the barriers she'd erected when the reality of their encounter had hit home. Instead, she put one foot in front of the other and headed for the door.

"Are you okay to drive?" he asked, a small frown of concern causing parallel lines to form between his brows. "I don't mind dropping you home. I can always bring your car to you tomorrow."

"No, I'll be all right. Thank you."

"You know, independence is fine and all that, but accepting help every now and then is okay, too."

"I know, and when I need help, I'll ask for it," she answered firmly.

She could feel the heat rolling gently from his body, bringing with it the leather and spicy wood scent of his cologne. It made her want to do something crazy, like nibble on the hard line of his jaw, or bury her nose in the hollow at the base of his throat. Man, she really needed to get out of here before she acted on those irrational thoughts.

"Thanks again for tonight," she said.

"You're welcome. We still have plenty more to discuss. Okay if I get in touch?"

She hesitated, wishing she could say no, and knowing she needed to say yes. Given the way he tugged at her, emotionally and mentally, she knew it wasn't going to be easy sharing a baby with him. Jenna settled for a quick nod and all but fled down the stairs. But he was right at her side, so that when she got to her car it was his hand that opened the door for her. He leaned down once she was settled inside.

"Red fluffy dice?" he asked with a chuckle when he saw the things dangling from the rearview mirror of her ever-so-practical station wagon.

"I have dreams of owning a red convertible one day. *Had* dreams," she corrected.

With the baby on the way, that was one dream that would have to be shelved for a while. Maybe even forever.

"Classic or new?" Dylan persisted.

"Classic, of course."

He gave her a wink. "That's my girl."

She felt an almost ridiculous sense of pride in his obvious approval, and forced herself to quash it. It didn't matter whether he approved of her dreams or not. They weren't going to happen, not now. She was doing her best to hold everything else together. Luxury items were exactly that: luxury. An extravagance that was definitely not in her current budget.

"Well, good night," she said, staring pointedly at his hand on the door.

To her surprise he leaned down and reached for her chin, turning her head to face him, before capturing her lips in an all too short, entirely too sweet kiss.

"Good night. Drive safe," he instructed as he swung her door closed.

Her hands were shaking as she started the car and then placed them on the wheel. As she drove around the turning loop to head down the driveway, she sought refuge in anger. He'd done it on purpose, just to prove his point about compatibility. The thing was, she *knew* they were compatible sexually. Now they had to be compatible as parents. Seemed to her they'd definitely missed a few steps along the way, and now there was no going back.

His proposal of marriage was preposterous. She sneaked a glance in her rearview mirror at the two-story house, fully lit up from the outside and looking as unattainable as she knew a long-term relationship with a man like Dylan Lassiter was, too. Jenna forced her eyes forward, to focus on the road ahead, and her future. One where she'd have to fight to keep Dylan Lassiter on the periphery if she hoped to keep her sanity.

By the time she rolled her car into her garage and hit the remote to make the door close behind her, she felt no better. Seeing Dylan again had just put her well-ordered world into turmoil. She'd had enough chaos to last a lifetime. It was why, when she'd been placed with Margaret Connell after her father was jailed, she'd put her head down and worked her butt off to fit in and to do things right. Mrs. Connell's firm but steady presence had been a rock to a fifteen-year-old teetering on the rails of a very unsteady life.

Mrs. Connell had not only provided a home for her, she'd provided a compass—one Jenna could live by for the rest of her life. The woman had also provided a sense of accountability, paying Jenna a wage for the hours she spent cleaning up in the florist shop after school and learning how to put together basic bouquets for people who came in off the street and wanted something quick and simple.

By the time Jenna had finished high school, she'd known exactly what she wanted to do. She'd put herself through business school, spending every spare hour she wasn't studying working in the flower store, which she'd eventually bought and made her own. Mrs. Connell was now enjoying a well-earned retirement in Palm Springs, secure in the knowledge that all her hard work, both with Jenna and the business, hadn't been in vain.

Jenna calculated the time difference between here and Palm Springs. It probably still wasn't too late to call Mrs. Connell, and she so desperately needed the guidance of someone else right now. Someone older and wiser. Someone stronger than she was. But that would mean disclosing how she'd gotten herself into this situation. Telling someone else about behavior that she wasn't terribly proud of. The last thing Jenna wanted to hear in her mentor's voice was disappointment.

She climbed out of her car, went inside the house and got ready for bed. For all that Dylan had said about wanting to be a part of everything, she'd never felt so alone in her life, nor so confused.

Would he be so keen, she wondered, if he knew exactly who she was and what her life had been like? It was hardly the stuff of Disney movies. Her father had come home from work one day when she was nine, to find Jenna alone after school—her mother having abandoned them to sail, from New Zealand and her family, with the outgoing tide and pursue her dream of being a singer on a cruise ship. He'd pulled up stakes by the time Jenna was ten, and taken her to his native U.S.A., where he'd told her again and again that they'd strike it lucky any time, and that happily-ever-after was just around the corner for them both.

Unfortunately, his idea of luck had been inextricably linked to fleecing older, vulnerable women of their wealth, and using his looks and charm to get away with it. Until one day he'd gone a step too far.

Jenna pushed the memory to the back of her mind, where it belonged. She'd learned the hard way what it meant to be an unwitting public figure, and how cruel the media could be. Given the Lassiter family profile, any relationship between her and Dylan would be bound to garner attention—attention she didn't want or need. For her own sake, and that of her unborn baby, she would do whatever it took to keep a low profile.

She slid between the 800-thread-count bed linens she'd happily picked up in a clearance sale, and smoothed her feet and legs over the silky soft surface. She might not be in his league financially, but she didn't do so badly. She could provide for her baby, who certainly wouldn't want for anything. So what if some of their possessions were a little care-worn or threadbare or—Jenna grimaced in the dark, remembering Dylan's reaction—secondhand. She would manage, and her private life would remain that way: private.

* * *

Dylan whistled cheerfully as he drove away from the classic car dealer, relishing the sensation of the wind ruffling his hair. The thrum of the V8 engine under the shiny red hood before him set up an answering beat in his blood. Today was a perfect day for a picnic and he had just the partner in mind to share it.

After swinging by the Grill to make sure everything was running smoothly, he put together some food and drink, checked the GPS on his phone and headed toward Jenna's address, which he'd happily plucked from a phone book. He was curious to see where she lived—where she'd planned to raise their baby. *Planned* being in the past tense, because now that he was on the scene, he didn't intend for them to live apart. All he needed to do was convince Jenna.

When he turned into her driveway he had to admit he was surprised at where she lived: it was a new neighborhood, the streets lined with modern homes. Skateboards, bikes and balls littered the front yards. He could see why she'd be comfortable here. Even though he hadn't seen anyone yet, there was a sense of community and projected longevity about the area.

He saw curtains in windows on either side of her house twitch as he turned off the ignition and sat a moment in the car. A smile played at his lips. Neighborhood watch, no doubt. It was good to know Jenna had people looking out for her when he wouldn't be.

Dylan got out of the car. He couldn't wait to see her face. He strode up the path that led to the front door and pressed the doorbell. Nothing. He waited a minute and tried again.

"You looking for someone?" A woman's voice came

from over the well-trimmed hedge on one side of Jenna's property.

"Yes, ma'am," he answered with a smile that wiped the distrustful look off her face in an instant. "Is Jenna home?"

The woman blushed prettily. "She's gardening out back. Just follow the path around the side of the house and you'll find her."

"Thank you."

Clearly, he'd passed muster. He jangled the car keys in his hand as he made his way around to the rear of the house. It only took a minute to find her. She knelt by a raised bed of roses, pulling vigorously at the weeds and dumping them in a bucket beside her.

"That looks suspiciously like hard work. Need a break?"

Jenna jumped at his voice and looked up, using the back of her hand to push a few loose strands of hair from her eyes.

"No, thank you. This job isn't going to do itself."

"Why don't you get someone else in to help?"

"Because first, I don't have money to throw around like that, and second, I enjoy it."

His eyes swept across her face, taking in the smear of dirt on her flushed cheek and the dark shadows that were painted beneath her eyes.

"If you tell me what to do, will you let me help for a while so I can take you out to play after we're done?"

She looked startled for a minute. "Seriously?"

"Yeah, of course I'm serious."

She pursed her lips a second, making him wish he could taste them again. Last night's chaste kiss had done nothing but ignite a desire for more.

"You don't really want to garden, do you."

It was a statement, not a question. He shrugged. "I'd be lying if I said I did. But I'll do what's necessary to achieve my objective."

Jenna narrowed her eyes. "And your objective is…?"

"Taking you out to lunch."

"I'm not dressed for lunch."

"That's okay, I prepared a picnic."

A wistful expression replaced the wariness in her eyes. "A picnic? I've never been on one of those."

He couldn't hide his shock. "Never?"

She shook her head.

"Then let me be the one to remedy that for you." He stepped closer and took her hand in his, stripping off her gardening glove before doing the same with the other hand. "The weeds will still be here when we get back."

"Unfortunately."

"Then worry about them later. Come with me," he coaxed. "Now."

For a second she chewed at her lower lip, her gaze fixed on her hand still held in his.

"Shouldn't you be at work? The grand opening's not all that far away now, is it?"

"No, it's not. I've already been by the Grill today. Everything's under control. Besides, I'm the boss—when I say I need a bit of time out, I take it. So, are you coming?"

"Okay. But let me freshen up first."

"No problem. I'll meet you out front."

As much as he was itching to step inside her small home, to see what things she'd chosen to surround herself with, he sensed he'd pushed enough for one day. That she'd agreed to come out on the picnic with him was a coup in itself, and he'd take that victory before reaching for the next one.

"Give me ten minutes, then," she said, already walking toward the screened back door.

"No problem. Take all the time you need."

The door slammed behind her and he took a moment to look around the garden. Here and there were splashes of color, interspersed among some midsize trees. It was a good backyard, as backyards went. But it wasn't where his kid would grow up playing. Kids needed space—and he'd be providing it. Eventually.

Inside Jenna quickly changed from her tattered and dirty gardening gear into a T-shirt and jeans. To her surprise, she couldn't fasten the top button on her jeans, which was something she'd been able to manage, barely, last week. That was one thing pregnancy definitely guaranteed—change, and plenty of it.

She washed her face and smoothed on some tinted moisturizer. It would probably be too much to apply her usual makeup, but she wasn't going out with Dylan without feeling at least a little in control. She attempted a quick brush of her hair, but it was impossible to smooth the tangles that a sleepless night had wrought, so instead she carelessly swept it up and secured it with a few pins, then tied a scarf around her head.

Surveying the results in the mirror, she allowed herself a grin of approval. Her T-shirt was long and loose-fitting, her bra made of sturdier material than last night's. She'd be fine.

It took only a few seconds to lock up and head out the front door, but the instant her feet hit the porch she came to an abrupt halt. There, in her driveway, sat the car that had featured in all her fantasies. It was as if Dylan had reached into her mind and extracted the information himself, she thought, as she surveyed the fire-engine-red Cadillac convertible with whitewall tires and the top down. It was her dream car—right down to the red fluffy dice, twins to her own, hanging in front.

Dylan straightened from where he leaned against the passenger door, and flashed her a smile.

"You like it?"

Jenna forced herself to walk toward him, still locked in a state of disbelief.

"I love it. What…? How…?" She shook her head. "Did you hire it for the day or something?"

"No," he said. "After you mentioned it last night I thought I'd look around online. I saw it this morning and bought it."

"You *bought* it? Just like that?"

He lifted the keys and dangled them in front of her face. "You want to drive?"

"Do I!" She snatched the set from his hand and tossed her bag in the back before racing around to the driver's side. She threw herself into the seat and ran her hands over the steering wheel and the dash. "I can't believe it. You really bought this today?"

Dylan seated himself next to her with another one of those smiles that made her insides melt. "Sure did. Shall we give her a run? I was thinking we could head out to the Crystal Lake Reservoir, find a nice spot and have our picnic."

It was at least a forty-minute drive to get there. She'd love every second of it.

"Let's get going then," she said, smiling back at him.

He stared at her, the smile on his face changing, his expression becoming more serious. He lifted a hand and touched her cheek with one finger.

"You're so beautiful, you know that?"

Jenna didn't know what to say. Her stomach clenched

in reaction to his touch, to his softly spoken words. She wanted to refute it, but at the same time wanted to hold those words in a safe place in the corner of her heart, forever.

Dylan let his hand drop, breaking the spell. "C'mon," he said, "let's get this show on the road."

The engine's powerful roar when it turned over sent a shiver of happiness up her spine.

"I still can't believe you bought this," she said as she backed out the drive and onto the street. "That's just so impulsive."

"Why shouldn't I?" He shrugged. "I bought it for you."

Six

Dylan watched as her expression turned from one of sheer glee to one of horror. She jammed on the brakes, throwing him slightly forward.

"Whoa, there. Easy on the brakes, sweetheart."

"Tell me you didn't do that."

"Didn't do what?"

"Buy me this car."

"If I did, I'd be lying."

"I can't accept it." She shook her head vehemently. "That's just crazy."

"It is what it is."

But he was walking on thin air. She was out of the car—leaving the engine still running, the driver's door open—and standing on the sidewalk, her arms wrapped around herself in protection as if warding off some terrible pain.

Dylan shot out of the car and closed in on her, but she put up her hands, halting him in his tracks. What had he done? He could see her shaking from here.

"What is it? What's wrong?"

"You're trying to buy me, aren't you?" Her voice quavered and her face was pale. "Trying to make me do what you want."

"Jenna, the car's a gift."

"Some bloody gift!" she snapped, her eyes now burning as she looked at him squarely. "I know what a car like that is worth. You don't just buy one in the morning and give it away by the afternoon."

"Jenna, I'm hardly a poor man. I want to see you have nice things."

"Why?"

He was confused. *"Why?"*

"Yes, why? Why me? Why now? As I said last night, we hardly know each other. We had sex *once.* We're having a baby. That's it. That's all there is to us, and now you're buying me a Cadillac?"

"Maybe I'm buying it just because I can. Maybe I need to prove to you that I can provide for you, that you don't need to do all this on your own, that you don't need to keep pushing me away. Yes, we're having a baby—*together.* I know we're doing this all back to front, but I want to get to know the mother of my kid. I want to see if we can be a couple."

Jenna's eyes flicked away from his, but not before he saw the sheen of tears reflected there. Before he could close the distance between them, the first drop spilled off a lash and tracked down her cheek. She lifted a hand and furiously scrubbed it, and those that followed, away.

"I don't want the car," she said adamantly, through clenched teeth. "I will not be bought."

"Fine. I'll take it back tomorrow. But can't we just enjoy today? Take it for a spin. Enjoy it while we can?"

He tentatively put his arms around her, pulling her closer. She lifted her chin and blinked away the moisture in her eyes. She was one tough chick, that was for sure.

"Just for today?" she asked, her voice tight.

"Sure, if that's what you want."

"So it's not mine anymore?"

"Nope."

He felt a pang of regret that he'd have to say goodbye to the big red beast, but if that's what it took to begin to win her trust, then that's what he'd do. Jenna looked past him at the car and he could see the longing in her gaze. Even though she wanted it, she would still refuse it. Her moral ground remained solid, even in the face of a desire so hungry she was almost salivating with it.

"Jen?" he said, noticing that he wasn't the only one with eyes on her right now. In fact, not only were curtains twitching, but there were faces appearing at windows, too.

"What?"

"I don't want to rush you, but shall we go? We're providing a bit of a show here."

"Oh, God," she groaned. Her lips firmed and she drew in a breath. "Fine, let's go then. But you can drive."

He didn't argue. Instead he guided her around to the passenger side of the car and helped her into her seat before closing the door and heading to the driver's side.

"You okay?" he said, reaching across the car to squeeze her hand.

"I'm fine. Just go, will you?"

"Whatever the lady wants."

The trip to the reservoir was accomplished in silence. Dylan kept throwing surreptitious looks at Jenna during the journey and was relieved to note the tension in her body had begun to ease as they headed out of Cheyenne. As they wound along the route that led to the reservoir he kept an eye out for a place with a vantage point overlooking the lake. He gave a grunt of satisfaction when he found just the spot, and brought the car to a stop beneath some trees.

Through a gap between the trunks, the lake gleamed like highly polished mirrored glass, reflecting the surrounding rock formations and flora in a perfect echo of their surroundings.

Dylan got out of the car and opened the trunk, unloading a large rubber-backed blanket and a picnic hamper. He passed the blanket to Jenna.

"Here, find us a spot. I'll bring the food and drinks."

She took it without a word and headed a little closer to the water. When he joined her she'd spread it out in a sunny spot in a small clearing.

"I...I'm sorry. For before," she said in a stilted tone. "I'm sure my reaction probably appeared over the top to you."

"A little, but that's okay. No apology needed."

"No," she said vehemently. "You were trying to be nice and I threw it back at you. I just..."

She averted her gaze out over the water, as if searching for something to draw strength from to help her get her words out. Dylan waited quietly, watching the internal battle reflected on her face.

"I just don't like it when people think they can buy someone else with things, or when other people accept them."

Dylan scratched his jaw as he played her words over in his mind. Sounded as if there was a story behind that statement. Would he ever hear it from her? He hoped so.

"Fair comment," he answered, putting the hamper and the small drinks cooler down at the edge of the blanket. "And duly noted for future reference."

"You're mad at me, aren't you?"

"Not mad. Disappointed, maybe, that you don't feel you can accept the car from me, but hey, I'm a big boy now. I'll get over it."

And, he added silently, *I'll find a way through that wall of yours, one day.*

He opened the cooler and handed Jenna a bottle of mineral water before snagging one for himself.

"Italian?" she asked, looking at the label. "Is there anything you do normally?"

"Define *normally*."

She chewed on her lower lip a moment before speaking. "Well, inexpensively, then."

"Why should I?"

"Because one day you might wish you had, for one. What if the bottom drops out of steak houses and the Lassiter Grill Corporation goes down with it?"

Dylan shook his head, a smile playing around his mouth. "It'll never happen. People like food, especially good food. Plus, they're more conscious these days of how their food is raised. The cattle on the Big Blue are free range and grass fed. Only nature's goodness. The beef served in the Grills is the best in the country, probably the world, and I ensure our staff and our dishes live up to that promise."

"You're very confident."

He paused a moment, thinking about it. "Yeah, I guess so. I haven't always been this way. Being raised by J.D. made a big difference, though. It took a while, but we got there."

"You lost your parents quite young, didn't you?"

"Sage was six and I was four. I don't remember too much about them, but Sage—" Dylan sighed "—he took it real hard. Kind of put himself in opposition to anything J.D. said or suggested from day one."

"I always wished I had a brother or sister," Jenna said wistfully, taking a sip of her water.

He found his gaze caught by her actions, riveted by the movement of her slender throat as she swallowed.

"Only child?"

"Only and lonely," she said lightly, but even so, he heard the truth behind her words.

"Where did you grow up?"

"All over. I was born in New Zealand and grew up there before my mom and dad broke up."

"New Zealand, huh? I thought you had a bit of an accent."

"Hardly," she snorted. "When we heard my mom had died, Dad packed us up and brought us back here to the States. Any accent soon got teased out of me at school."

"Back to the States?"

"My father's American. We traveled a bit and eventually I got to settle here in Cheyenne. The rest, as they say, is history."

Painful history by the sound of things. What she didn't say spoke louder than what she did. Dylan turned to the hamper in a bid to break the somber mood that had settled over them. He reached past the cooling pads he'd packed around the food and lifted out a couple covered containers. He popped the lids off, revealing in one, sandwiches made with freshly baked whole grain bread, and in the other, a selection of sliced fruit.

"I can promise you I prepared these myself and that I carefully studied what you can and can't eat in pregnancy," he said, putting the dishes down between them on the blanket.

Jenna picked up a sandwich and studied the filling. "You mean you washed and dried the lettuce in here yourself?"

"With my own fair hands," he assured her with a grin. "But don't tell any of my kitchen staff that or they'll expect me to do everything myself."

They ate in companionable silence and Dylan quietly cleared up when they were done.

"Tell me why you've never been on a picnic before," he suggested, interrupting her contemplation of the lake's beauty.

She remained silent for a while, and so still he began to wonder if she'd even heard him.

"I guess I just never had the opportunity before," she eventually said, but he could tell she was leaving plenty out of that trite little answer. "It's nice, though. Thank you."

He'd have to be satisfied with that, he told himself, and filled in the gap in conversation that followed with his own tales of the times he and Sage had raided their aunt's kitchen to take a picnic outdoors. He loved it when he made Jenna laugh. It lifted the shadows from her eyes and showed a different side to her than the one that constantly met him head-on and tried to thwart his every attempt to spoil her.

It wasn't much later that Jenna lay down in the sunshine and closed her eyes. She was asleep in seconds. The day's temperature was still pretty mild, but the wind had a bite in it, so Dylan got his sweater from the trunk of the car and gently put it over her as she slept.

He stretched out beside her, wishing they had the kind of relationship where he could pull her into his arms, curl around her body and keep her warm with his heat alone.

All in good time, he assured himself. All in good time.

Jenna woke with a shiver as a shadow passed over the sun. She opened her eyes to see a cloud sailing overhead. She realized that she had something covering her and lifted it to see what it was. Dylan's sweater? When had he done that? A warm sensation filled her at his consideration.

For a minute or two she just lay there, absorbing the

sounds of the insects and birds, and relishing the peaceful surroundings, before she became aware of a deep steady breathing that came from close by. She turned her head and saw Dylan lying on his back beside her. Well, that answered one question, she thought. He didn't snore. His arms were bent up under his head and even in sleep the latent strength of his biceps were obvious. She observed the steady rise and fall of his chest. His T-shirt had risen above the waistband of his jeans, exposing just a hint of his lower belly.

At the sight of his bare flesh a tingle washed through her, and her fingertips itched to reach out—to touch and trace that line of flesh with the faint smattering of dark hair. She didn't dare give in to the temptation, though. Things were already incendiary between them. They didn't need any further complications and right now, to her, a relationship with Dylan was a complication she'd rather avoid.

She looked past him to the Caddy, sitting in all its shiny glory under the trees.

What kind of man did that? she asked herself. Who on earth bought a classic car on a whim for someone he barely knew from Adam, just because she said it was a dream of hers? The thought triggered a memory of the day her dad had come to pick her up from junior high. They were living in Seattle at the time and he'd rolled up in a brand-new 5-series BMW, looking like a cat that got the cream.

Soon after, she'd met the reason behind the car. His latest conquest had bought it for him when he'd admired it one day as they'd passed a dealership. It was payment, he'd said flippantly, for services rendered. Jenna hadn't fully understood, at the time, just what he'd meant by that. Just as she'd never understood, until she got older, why all the women he dated had at least ten, sometimes more, years on him. Or why he was always turning up with expensive things. Even back then it had made her uncomfortable. It hadn't seemed right, especially when her dad never appeared to hold down a real job. But her father had just laughed off her concerns when she got brave enough to broach them.

He'd never stayed with anyone for long. All of a sudden she'd wake one morning and they'd be on the move again. Sometimes clear across the country in pursuit of his next happily-ever-after. She'd had no idea that even while he was dating one woman, he was casually grooming up to five others via the internet. Nor did she know that when they'd moved to Laramie when she was fifteen, and she'd shaved her head as part of a school-run fund-raiser for one of their cancer-stricken teachers, that her father would use that picture to create a whole new set of lies to fleece his victims with.

Lies that eventually saw him hauled off to jail for fraud and caused her to be placed here in Cheyenne with Margaret Connell. Jenna squeezed her eyes shut. She didn't want to think about that time—about the gross invasion of her life by the media, the reporters who'd accused her of being complicit in her father's schemes. She'd been just a kid, with nowhere and no one else to turn to. When child services had taken her, she'd wondered if she was going to end up in prison, too. After all, she had no one else. Her mother was dead. They'd learned she'd died less than a year after she'd left them, choking on her meal aboard ship. And there'd been no other family to come in and pick up Jenna's fractured life.

Mrs. Connell had been a much-needed anchor and a comfort. For the first time in her life Jenna had been able to stay in one place for more than what felt like five minutes. It hadn't broken her reticence about making friends, though. Even now she found it a struggle to get close to anyone. She'd learned growing up that it was better that way, better than having to say heart-wrenching goodbyes every time her life turned topsy-turvy again.

She studied Dylan's strong features. Even in sleep he looked capable, secure in his world. What would it be like to take a chance on him? To just go with the flow and let him take control of her and the baby's worlds?

Even as she considered it, the idea soured in her mind. And what about when he lost interest and moved on? she asked herself. As her father had moved on so many times? As Dylan himself had moved on from various publicly touted relationships in his life? She wouldn't do that to her child, or to herself. They were both worth so much more than that.

Self-worth. It was a hard lesson to learn, but it was one Margaret Connell had reinforced every day Jenna had lived under her roof. It was why Jenna could never accept anything that was a facsimile of a real life, or a real love. She'd been there already and she still bore those scars. Probably always would.

Dylan's eyes flicked open and he turned his head to look at her. "Nice sleep?" he asked with a teasing smile.

"Mmm, it was lovely. Thank you for this. It was a great idea."

"Even though we had to do it in that?" He nodded over toward the Cadillac.

"Yes." She heaved a mock long-suffering sigh. "Even though we had to do it in that."

He rolled onto his side, facing her. "You certain you don't want it? You're allowed to change your mind, y'know."

"No, thank you. I don't want it. Besides, there's no anchor point for an approved child restraint," she said soberly, reminded anew of how much her life, her dreams, would change in a few short months' time.

"Good point. Maybe I'll keep it for date nights."

Jenna felt her entire body revolt at the statement. Here she was contemplating approved child restraints for *their* baby, and he was busily planning his next night out with some woman.

"*Our* date nights," he specified with a wicked grin that told her he knew exactly what she'd been thinking.

"We won't be having any of those," she said in an attempt to suppress his humor, especially since it was humor at her expense.

"I think it would be good for our kid to see our common interests don't just revolve around him or her. I've seen too many couples lose sight of what they feel for one another when they're crazy busy with their kids and with work. They lose themselves, and worse, they lose each other."

His words, spoken so simply, ignited a yearning inside her that made her heart ache. He made it sound so simple. But she knew to the soles of her feet that life just wasn't like that.

"You're forgetting one thing," she murmured. "We aren't a couple."

He leaned a little closer. "We could be."

And with that, he inched a tiny bit nearer and closed his lips on hers.

Seven

The second their lips touched, Dylan knew it was a mistake. If only because they were in a public place and there was no way he could take this all the way. Not here, not right now—even though his body demanded he do so. He should have waited until they were behind closed doors. Someplace where they could relish their privacy and take the time to explore one another fully. Enjoy one another without fear of discovery.

It didn't mean he couldn't make the most of the moment, though, and he slid his hand under Jenna's head, cradling her gently as he sipped at the nectar of her mouth. Her lips were soft and warm, pliant beneath his. A rush of need burst through what was left of his brain, urging him to coax, to plunder, to take this so much further than a kiss. But he held back.

He wanted her, there was no denying it. But he was prepared to take this slowly—as painful as that would be—if that was what he had to do to convince her he was serious.

Jenna's hands lifted up to bracket his face, and he took that as permission to use his mouth to tease her some more—to open her up and taste her, their tongues meshing, their teeth bumping. How he wished he could see all of her, and touch and taste every inch.

She was pregnant with his child and he'd never seen her naked. Just the idea of it made his nerves burn with raging heat, and urged him to go further. But still he held back, eventually forcing himself to ease away, to create at least a hand span of distance between them. It wasn't enough. There could be an entire continent between them and it wouldn't deaden how he felt about her. How much he wanted her.

"Think about it," he said, rolling away and standing up.

"Think about what?" she asked, looking up at him with a dazed expression in her eyes.

He fought back a smile. Maybe that's all he'd have to do to convince her they should get married. Kiss her senseless until she simply said yes.

He offered her a hand and helped her to her feet, then picked up and folded the blanket, slinging it over one arm. "Us. Together. You know—a couple."

She started to shake her head, but he reached up and gently took her chin between his fingers.

"Think about it, Jenna. At least give me a chance to prove to you how good we could be together. Not just as lovers, although I know that will take us off the Richter scale—again. But as a couple." His hand dropped to the slight mound of her belly. "As a family."

Before she could respond, he grabbed the cooler and turned and walked to the car. He didn't want to see rejection in her eyes. Not when he'd realized, even as he spoke, just how much he wanted this. He'd lost his parents when he was only four, Aunt Ellie—his adoptive mother—only three years after that. He was luckier than most. He'd had four parents in his lifetime, five when he counted Marlene as well, and each one had left an imprint of devotion. An imprint so indelible it had made him promise himself that, when he eventually had a family, he would be a part of his children's lives. They would know the security of parents who loved them unreservedly. He'd had that, and he would walk over flaming gas ranges if necessary, to make sure his kid had it, too.

Jenna appeared beside him, handing him the now empty hamper as he stowed the cooler and blanket in the trunk.

"Will you at least consider it?" he asked, closing the trunk with a solid thud.

She looked up at him, vulnerability reflecting starkly at him from those dark brown eyes of hers. "Okay."

One small word and yet it had the power to change everything about the life he lived, about the choices he'd made. It should be daunting and yet it made him feel excited on a level he hadn't anticipated. Made him almost feel a sense of relief that he could, maybe, stop searching for that one ephemeral thing that he'd always felt was missing from a life rich in so much already. The thing he'd sought in travel and women and had yet to find. He shoved his hands in his jeans pockets to hold himself back, to stop himself from giving in to the impulse to grab her and twirl her around with a whoop of satisfaction.

"Thank you."

The drive back to her home was completed in silence but it was a comfortable one. With one hand on the wheel, he'd reached across and tangled his fingers in hers for most of the journey. It wasn't something he'd ever stopped to consider before with anyone else but, right now, he felt as if the connection between Jenna and him had solidified just that bit more. And it felt strangely right. By the time he dropped her off and saw her into her house he was already formulating plans for tomorrow. Plans that most definitely featured Jenna Montgomery.

Monday morning, the smell of fresh paint and new carpet filled Dylan's nose the moment he strode in through the front door to check on progress at the restaurant and was pleased to see the delivery of the new furniture was well under way. He stopped a second to inhale the newness, the potential that awaited. The excitement that had thrummed quietly inside of him built to new levels. It was happening. He'd felt excited about each of the previous three Lassiter Grills to date but this one was even more special to him than the others.

Hard on the heels of his excitement came a thrust of regret that J.D. couldn't be here to see their dreams become a reality. It was still hard to accept that his larger-than-life, hard-as-nails father figure was really gone. At moments like this, it was that much worse.

God, but he missed that man. And as much as he grieved for J.D. with a still-raw ache, he owed it to the old man to make sure that everything about this new restaurant would match, if not eclipse, their existing venues. That meant keeping up his hands-on approach to business and proving that J.D.'s faith in making him CEO of the Lassiter Grill Corporation was well founded.

With a nod of approval, he walked past the massive polished wood bar to the double doors that led into the kitchen. As much as he loved the front of the restaurant, this was the hub of what made the Lassiter Grills great. This was where he belonged, amongst the stainless steel countertops and the sizzle and steam and noisy organized chaos of cooking. The last of the equipment had been installed a week ago and his team had spent the past week trialing the signature dishes that would be specific to the Cheyenne steak house, along with the much loved menu that made the Lassiter Grills so popular in L.A., Las Vegas and Chicago.

It was ironic, Dylan thought as he surveyed the hand-picked team, that he'd spent the better part of his adult years running away from responsibility and family commitment and yet in the past five years he'd embraced every aspect of both of those things. Clearly, he was ready to settle down.

The very idea would have sent a chill through him not so long ago but over the past few months, well, it had tickled at the back of his mind over and over again. Maybe it was losing J.D. so suddenly that had made him begin to question his own mortality and his own expectations of life. Or maybe he was finally, at the age of thirty-five, mature enough to accept there was more to life than the hedonistic whirlwind that had been his world to date. It was a sobering thought.

Satisfied that his staff had it all under control, he drove over to Jenna's store. He pushed the door open and stepped in, his nostrils flaring at the totally different scents in the air, compared to those back at the Grill. As before, there was no one in the front of the store, but he could hear off-key humming coming from out back. The humming came closer and he saw Jenna walking through, carrying an armload of bright fresh daisies. She'd pulled her hair into a ponytail today, lifting it high off her face and exposing her cheekbones and the perfectly shaped shells of her ears. He imagined taking one of those sweet lobes between his teeth and his body stirred in instant response.

"Oh, I didn't hear you come in," she said, placing the flowers on the main counter.

"No problem. I haven't been waiting long."

He studied her carefully. She looked tired, a little pale.

As if she'd had about as much trouble getting to sleep last night as he had. He couldn't help himself; he lifted a hand and skimmed the back of his fingers across her cheek.

"You okay? You're not overdoing things, are you?"

She pulled away from his touch. "I'm fine, Dylan. Trust me, I won't do anything to harm this baby. I may not have planned for it, but now that it's a reality, there's nothing I want more in my life."

There was a fierce undertone to her voice that convinced him she was telling the truth. It didn't stop him worrying, especially when she bent to shift a large container filled with water to another spot on the floor.

"Here," he said, brushing her aside. "Let me do that for you. I thought you had staff to help you."

Jenna stood back, a quizzical expression on her face. "I do, but they're part-time. I open and close the store each day."

"Then let me do the heavy stuff today."

"No problem, but I'll be back to doing it again tomorrow. Unless you plan on being here for me every morning to help me rearrange everything in the store?

"If that's what it takes," he said as he straightened. "Or I could arrange that you had someone here first and last thing to do this if you'd rather."

She shook her head, a rueful smile pulling at those kissable lips of hers. "I'd prefer to do it myself."

"Hey, can you blame me for wanting to take care of you? You're carrying precious cargo there."

A wistful expression settled on her face. "Yeah, I am, aren't I? But I still have a job to do. Now, I guess you're here to see what I've worked out for the flowers for the opening? I've sketched a few ideas and also thought I'd put something together quickly with what I had out back."

She grabbed a square of burlap and some twine, and

wrapped them around a plastic-lined cardboard base. She then moved around the store, selecting stems of greenery and laying them on the counter next to the daisies. Before his eyes, she used the assortment of items to create a vision of beauty.

"Hmm, needs some berries, too, I think," she muttered, more to herself than anything. A second or two later she turned the arrangement around to face him. "There, what do you think?"

He eyed the compilation of color and texture and decided he liked it very much. She had a genuine talent for this. There was nothing generic about what she'd created. She'd taken his minimal instructions and put together what he'd wanted without his fully understanding it himself.

"That's great. So these would be for the tables?"

She nodded. "And then I'd do something bigger, maybe in a crate propped on some hay bales, in the foyer. What do you think?"

"I think you're an artist."

She gave a little shrug. "I have a knack, I guess."

"Don't sell yourself short, Jenna." Dylan cast his eye over the arrangement again. "I'm thinking, though, that the colors need to be bolder. These might disappear in the decor. Why don't you come back with me to the restaurant for lunch? You can get a better feel of what I mean."

"You're going to feed me again? Three times in three days? This is getting to be a habit."

"We need live subjects to try the menu, and some of our waitstaff need the experience, too," he explained, even though it was more a case of now that he'd seen her again, he didn't want to let her out of his sight. "You'd be doing me a favor."

He didn't fool her for a second, that much was obvious

from the smile that spread across her face. "A favor, huh? Well, since one of my workers is due in shortly, I think I'd be able to slip away for an hour for lunch."

"Just an hour?"

"I do have a business to run. Besides, won't it be better for your team to get used to working with customers who are in a hurry?"

"Good point," he acceded, even though he wished he could just whisk her away for the afternoon and keep her to himself.

"I'll come at one, okay? I have some orders I need to put together for our delivery guy and—" she glanced at her wristwatch "—I need to get to work on them now if they're to be ready on time."

"That's great. I'll be waiting."

Jenna watched him leave, surprised at herself for agreeing to lunch today. Despite all her tossing and turning last night, and her resolve to try and keep things purely business between them, it appeared she wanted to see him again more than she'd realized. True, this visit was under the guise of checking the decor of the restaurant, but the prospect of spending more time with him, even if only an hour, made her bubble inside, as if the blood in her veins was carbonated.

Valerie, her assistant, came in through the front door.

"Wow, tell me the guy just leaving wasn't an apparition."

"Oh, no." Jenna smiled. "He's quite real."

"Just my luck to be running late today, or I could've served him."

Jenna looked at her long-married friend, a mother of four, and raised a brow. "Seriously?"

"Well, a girl's entitled to her dreams, isn't she? He

looks vaguely familiar. What did he want? Please tell me he wasn't ordering flowers for his girlfriend."

"That was Dylan Lassiter," Jenna said with a laugh, "and he's ordering flowers, through us, for the latest Lassiter Grill opening."

"He is? Wow, that's got to be good for business. You think they'll keep us as a regular florist? It'd be a fabulous lift for our profile."

"I haven't discussed future work with him, but we have a good start. Which reminds me, if I don't get my work out of the way this morning, I won't be able to make it to the restaurant for our next meeting at one."

"I could always go for you," Valerie suggested with a wink.

"I'm sure you could," Jenna said, still laughing, and imagining Dylan's face if she took Valerie up on her offer. But an unexpected surge of possessiveness filled her. She didn't want anyone handling Dylan's requests but herself. Dragging her thoughts together, she briskly continued, "C'mon, help me with these orders before Bill gets here for pickup."

The balance of the morning flew by. While she worked, Jenna considered the ramifications of having a regular corporate account with the Lassiter Grill. The exposure for her business would be great, there was no denying it. She made a mental note to raise the subject with Dylan, and went to get ready for their lunch date.

She was running late by the time she arrived at the restaurant but luckily found a parking space just around the corner.

Dylan was waiting by the front door as she jogged up the sidewalk.

"I was beginning to think you'd stood me up," he said, opening the door for her and guiding her inside.

"Just a busy morning, that's all."

"We have company for lunch. My brother, Sage, is joining us, together with his fiancée, Colleen."

Jenna immediately felt at a disadvantage. "Oh, I wish you'd said so. I'm not dressed for company."

Dylan turned his gaze to her and she felt him assess her from top to toe. "You look mighty fine from where I'm standing."

Heat bloomed in her chest and flooded all the way up to her cheeks. Great, now she'd look like a little red fire engine when introduced to his family.

"I mean it, Dylan," she said awkwardly.

"So do I. Seriously, you have nothing to worry about. They're my family and they'll love you any way you're dressed."

He grabbed her hand and led her inside. Her eyes darted around the dining room, taking in the design features that were such an integral part of the pictures she'd seen of each Lassiter Grill. While the building had a stone exterior, the interior walls were log lined. Her eyes roamed over the high ceilings, hung with massive iron fans, and down to the wooden plank floors. A huge floor-to-ceiling stone fireplace held a place of dominance in the center of the restaurant. What they'd sacrificed in space they'd more than made up in character. She loved the ranch-style atmosphere. It was realistic without being over the top. An idea popped into her head.

"I've been thinking about the opening and about how you'll dress the tables for the night," she began.

"Uh-huh?"

"What do you think of burlap table runners on white linen?"

He paused a moment, considering. "That sounds like a good idea. D'you have pictures of what you're thinking?"

She nodded.

"Good, we can talk about them after lunch. C'mon over and meet my brother."

Her nerves assailed her and she tugged at Dylan's hand, making him stop and turn to face her.

"Do they know?"

"Know?"

"About us, about the baby."

"Not yet. Do you want to tell them?"

She shook her head vehemently. It was enough that Dylan knew, but she wasn't ready to share the news with others.

"Okay, but they're going to find out sooner or later," he warned.

"Just not yet, okay?"

They crossed to the table where the couple were seated. Sage rose to his feet as they approached. Slightly taller than his brother, with medium brown hair sprinkled with a touch of gray at the temples, he looked like a man used to being in control. He also didn't seem like the type you could hide anything from for long, and the way his gaze dropped to her hand clasped in Dylan's larger one, and then back to his brother's face, told her he saw a great deal more than what lay on the surface. She pulled free of Dylan's grip as a frisson of unease wended its way down her spine. She so wasn't ready for this.

"Jenna, this is my brother, Sage, and his fiancée, Colleen. Sage, Colleen, this is Jenna Montgomery."

"Pleased to meet you," Jenna said, taking the bull by the horns and stepping forward with her hand outstretched. "Dylan's asked my firm to do the flowers for the opening. I hope you don't mind my crashing your lunch, but he wanted me to see the restaurant before we confirmed a color palette."

She knew, as soon as the words left her mouth, that she'd overcompensated. As if sensing her discomfort, Colleen rose from her chair with a welcoming smile and shook Jenna's hand.

"I'm pleased to meet you. Didn't you do the flowers for—"

"Angelica's rehearsal dinner, yes," Dylan interrupted, his swift interjection earning him a curious glance from his brother.

"I was going to say for a friend of mine's dinner party a couple of weeks ago," Colleen corrected smoothly, still holding Jenna's hand. "She was thrilled with what you did. I know you'll do a great job for Dylan."

Jenna began to feel herself relax as Colleen took over the conversation. It didn't mean that Sage stopped his perusal of her, but she allowed his fiancée to distract her as they turned the discussion to the pair's upcoming wedding and what the best flowers and style of bouquet might be. Across the square table, Dylan and his brother bent their heads together in deep discussion. Despite the differences in their coloring, their eyes were very much the same and the shape of their jaw and their mannerisms spoke of their strong familial connection.

Dylan looked up and flashed Jenna a smile before shifting his attention back to his brother, and she felt herself relax a little more. Colleen was very easy to talk to, and by the time they'd ordered off the menus and awaited their meals, Jenna found herself beginning to enjoy the other couple's company. Sage, while appearing a little standoffish at first, was clearly very much in love with his fiancée, and Jenna had to quell a pang of envy.

What would it have been like to meet Dylan and let a relationship with him progress the way most normal couples started? She shoved the thought aside for the piece of mental candy floss it was. She couldn't afford to indulge in thoughts of what might have been. She had been dealt large doses of reality in her lifetime, and coping with those, while keeping her wits about her, was paramount.

When their orders came Jenna applied herself vigorously to her serving of smoked baby back ribs with fries and grilled corn on the cob, which certainly beat a hasty sandwich grabbed in between customers at her shop. It felt strange being the only diners in a restaurant, waited on so industriously by the staff there, although the other three seemed to take it in stride. Jenna took her cue from Dylan and tried to act as if she was used to this kind of thing.

About thirty minutes later, when Sage made his apologies and rose to leave the table, Jenna decided she should do the same.

"No, wait for me here while I see Sage and Colleen out," Dylan insisted. "We still have those colors to discuss, as well as the table dressing you mentioned."

She nodded and turned her attention to the glass of mineral water Dylan had ordered for her. The water reminded her she needed to find the restroom. She got up and moved to the front of the restaurant, but before she could reach the facilities she overheard Sage talking to his brother.

"She's pregnant, Dylan. I hope you know what you're doing."

"I know she's pregnant. It's my baby."

"It's what?" Sage couldn't hide the shock in his voice.

"It's my baby and I'm going to marry her."

"Don't be a fool, man. It's not like you were even dating. You don't *know* her or anything about her. You don't even know for sure if the baby's yours—it could be anyone's. Shouldn't you at least wait until it's born, so you can do a paternity test?"

The sour taste of fear filled Jenna's mouth. This was exactly what she'd hoped to avoid. She didn't need Sage's censure or his implications. Yes, she had behaved like a tramp that Friday evening back in March. But so had Dylan. It was unfair that there was always one set of rules for guys and then another for women. The fact remained that they were dealing with the outcome of their dalliance, but the last thing she wanted was for it to become common knowledge. Not when she'd worked so hard, for so long, to wash away the taint of her father's behavior from her life.

She was where she was and who she was despite her upbringing. And, dammit, she would make a great mother even if juggling her business and motherhood would be a challenge. Jenna knew, to her cost, that life wasn't about easy solutions. It was about making the right choices and working hard to hold on to them.

"I don't like your insinuation, brother. Be very careful what you say about Jenna. I plan to marry her and I will raise my kid with her."

Dylan's tone brooked no argument and Jenna's spirits lifted to hear him defend her.

"Look, I didn't mean to offend you, but let's be realistic about this. At least have her investigated. If you won't, I will."

Ice cold sensation spilled through her veins. Investigation? It wouldn't take much to unearth her past, a past she'd fought hard to put behind her. Dylan's voice was raised when he answered his brother.

"I am being realistic about this, Sage. You know what family means to me. You know what *you* mean to me. I am not walking away from my son or daughter, and I'm not walking away from Jenna."

She held her breath through the tense silence that developed between the brothers, but she couldn't help but shift slightly. She really needed to pee. Her movement must have made some sound, because Dylan turned his head, his eyes spearing her where she stood.

"Um, I was just looking for the restrooms?" she said, horribly uncomfortable that she'd been caught standing there, eavesdropping.

"Through there," he said, pointing.

She scurried in the direction he'd indicated. After she relieved herself, she washed her hands under cold water, and then assessed her reflection in the mirror. She'd faced condemnation before and survived. It wasn't pretty, but she'd do it again if she had to. She dried her hands and returned to the restaurant. Dylan stood waiting for her.

"I'm sorry you had to hear that."

"It's okay. It's only what everyone will think, anyway." She brushed it off, but a note of how she was feeling must have crept into her voice.

"Jenna, I—"

"Look, let's just leave it, okay? Thank you for lunch. Now that I've been here I think I'll have a better idea about what you'll need for the floral designs, and I agree, bold and strong colors will be best." She flicked a look at her wristwatch. "I need to get back to the store."

"What about the other matters we were going to discuss?" he asked, searching her eyes. But she found herself unwilling to meet his.

"I'll email you."

"That sounds suspiciously like a brush-off." He cupped her shoulders with his big strong hands, the warmth of them swiftly penetrating the thin knit jacket and silk blouse she wore. "I'm not giving up on us, Jenna."

"Dylan, there is no *us*."

"I refuse to accept that," he said succinctly. "And one thing you need to know about me is that when something or someone is important to me, I never give up. You are important to me, Jenna Montgomery. Don't doubt it for a second."

When had anyone ever said anything like that to her before and meant it? She'd tried these past few days to keep Dylan at a distance, emotionally at least, but those few words wedged a tiny crack in the shell that had formed around her heart and began to split it apart. And when he lowered his face to hers, and caught her lips with his own, she felt herself reaching up to meet him halfway, as needy as a flower seeking rain on a drought-parched prairie. Wanting his promises, wanting his attention as she'd never wanted anything from anyone before.

Eight

Two days later Dylan paced the confines of his L.A. office. He was restless. Something had shifted inside him last Monday at the new restaurant. From the second he'd seen Sage take in Jenna's presence at his side and come to the correct conclusion about her pregnancy, he'd known he would defend her to anyone for any reason. For all time.

During his training in France he'd heard people refer to a *coup de foudre*—love at first sight—and he'd eschewed it for the fantastical notion it was. But thinking about that split second when he'd first noticed Jenna back in March, it was the only way to describe how he'd felt and behaved that night. It certainly described how he felt now. His family would just have to struggle to understand. Hell, even he struggled to get a grip on just how much one woman could turn his world upside down.

Since he'd walked back into her world five days ago, his every thought had been consumed by her, his every action taken with her in mind. Now, instead of focusing on the business and meetings to discuss the commencement of their planned East Coast expansion that had called him back to L.A., he was resenting the fact that it had taken him away from Cheyenne—away from Jenna.

He'd called her last night, but he'd sensed a reserve in her again, as if overhearing Sage's words had somehow erected an invisible wall thwarting the tentative connection they'd been building on. If only Dylan hadn't been forced to let her leave on Monday. If only he'd been able to pursue that kiss they'd shared at the restaurant just a little further. Instead, she'd all but fled from him and he'd had to let her go, his cell phone ringing in his pocket even as he watched her flee.

It was as if she was too scared to trust him, too scared to allow him into her life. But there was more to it than that. So many more layers to Jenna Montgomery that his hands itched to peel away. He'd have to bide his time, though, at least until Saturday, when he was due back in Cheyenne.

Dylan came to a halt at his office window and looked down over the sprawling metropolis that was Los Angeles. This had been his home, his city, for the past five years, and he'd fit in here. After training and cooking in restaurants in continental Europe and the United Kingdom, he'd been ready to come back to the States, ready to take on his next role in his career. But with J.D.'s death he'd been forced to take stock, to reevaluate his belief system and what was important in his life.

Right now, he missed Cheyenne. More to the point, he missed a certain woman who lived there. The perfect solution would be to take her and simply transplant her here into his life, his world. But even he knew that wouldn't be fair to her. She had a life in Cheyenne, a business and a home. Until he'd shown up in her store, she'd had everything worked out quite perfectly, Dylan had no doubt.

He forced his mind back to work, back to the task at hand. He'd get through these days because he had to, and because, ultimately, doing so would let him return to where he most wanted to be right now.

His phone chirping in his breast pocket was a welcome interruption to the frustration of his thoughts.

"Lassiter," he answered, without checking the caller I.D.

"Hey, Dylan, it's Chance. How are you?"

"I'm good, thanks, and you? How're things at the Big Blue?" Dylan smiled as he spoke. A call from his cousin was always a welcome break from everything else.

"I'm thinking of putting a barbecue together for Saturday. Think you could handle someone else's cooking for a change?"

Dylan laughed out loud. "Sure. For you, anything."

"Great. I was also thinking you might have a certain someone you'd like to bring along with you?"

"You been talking to Sage?"

"I might have."

Dylan could hear the smirk that was undoubtedly on his cousin's face.

"Chance—" he said, a grim note of warning in his voice.

"Hey, I promise I'll be on my best behavior, truly. I just want to meet her."

"And if she doesn't want to come?"

"I guess I can probably feed you, anyway," Chance drawled teasingly as if doing so would be a great hardship.

"That's big of you."

"But I'm sure, with your charm and skills, you'll manage to get her to come along."

"I'll let you know. What time do you want us?"

"Let's make it early. Hannah is visiting with her little girl, Cassie. She's the cutest tyke."

Since the discovery that Chance had a half sister—his father's secret daughter—the family had been getting to know one another, with great results. Now Hannah was engaged to Logan Whittaker, the lawyer who had been responsible for finding her when the contents of J.D.'s will had become known, and their family continued to expand. It was a good thing, Dylan thought privately.

"You getting ready to settle down, cuz?" It was Dylan's turn to tease now.

"Not likely," Chance replied, "but it's hard not to love her. She's a good kid. Anyway, come around six."

Dylan did a little mental calculation. By the time Jenna closed shop on Saturday and he picked her up, they could just about make it.

"We might be a little late," he said, "but we'll be there."

"Great, I'll let Mom know. She loves having family over. The more the merrier, right?"

Right, Dylan thought grimly as he disconnected the call. Now all he had to do was convince Jenna she wanted to meet more of his family, when all they probably wanted to do was subject her to the third degree. Damn Sage and his flapping mouth. Still, when push came to shove, his family was the backbone of who he was today, and Dylan wanted Jenna to see that, to be a part of it and to want their baby to be a part of it also. This gave her a perfect opportunity to see just what his family's lives were like.

Dylan had never been happier to leave L.A. and take the flight that brought him back to Cheyenne. As he pulled up in his SUV outside Jenna's house, he saw her at the front door before he could even get out of the car. He'd toyed with bringing the Caddy—he hadn't quite been able to bring himself to part with it just yet—but he knew it would probably make her uncomfortable. Besides, with the temperatures tonight set to drop to around fifty degrees, they'd probably welcome the climate control in the SUV instead.

He got out from behind the wheel and walked around to open her door for her, his eyes drinking in her appearance. He hadn't seen her for four days, but it felt like four weeks. Was it his imagination or was her tummy just that tiny bit rounder, her breasts that much fuller? Everything inside him tightened up a notch.

"Hi," she said, ducking her head as if she was a little shy.

"Hi back," he replied, bending his head to kiss her on the cheek. She blushed a pale pink when he did. He loved that he could do that to her, unnerve her like that. "I missed you."

She flicked her gaze up toward him and he saw her bite her lip, an action that sent heat rushing to his groin.

"I missed you, too."

She sounded puzzled by the fact and it made him quirk his lips in a smile. Dylan handed her into her seat and closed the door, suppressing the urge to punch the air and give a primal whoop of satisfaction. Progress. At last he was making progress.

He filled the time during their thirty-mile drive out to the Big Blue with what he'd been doing in L.A.

"So your sister lives in the house in L.A., too?"

"Yeah. Dad bought the property about twenty years ago and Angelica has really made it her own. She has a knack for decorating, for making a place feel like a home." He sighed inwardly. "It's always good to see her, but she's been pretty angry since Dad died. Things are strained between all of us."

"Angry?"

"Yeah." Dylan suddenly wished he hadn't brought the

subject up, but it probably deserved airing. "Dad was pretty old-fashioned, but I always thought he was fair. What he did to her when he left a controlling share in Lassiter Media to her fiancé, rather than to her, was a slap in the face. It's really upset her, especially since she'd basically been the one running Lassiter Media up until J.D.'s heart attack."

"Wow, I can see why she'd be upset. Is that why the wedding got called off?"

Dylan nodded. It still made him sick to his stomach. "Lassiter Media was Angelica's life, and now she's left wondering if the whole reason Evan asked her to marry him was so he could gain control of the company. Not exactly the basis for a good start to marriage."

Jenna was quiet for the rest of the journey, until Dylan reached across the center console and laced his fingers through hers.

"You okay?" he asked, flicking her a glance.

"Just a bit nervous."

"Don't be. Chance is a great guy."

"Who else will be there?"

"His mom, Marlene—she'll love you, don't worry. And his half sister, Hannah, is visiting with her daughter, Cassie. And look, we're nearly there."

He pulled in through the gates to what had, in his mind, always been home. After his parents died, J.D. and Ellie had brought him and Sage here to the ranch. Originally, the main house had been far more modest, but as the Big Blue had become more successful, it was replaced by the two-story wood-and-metal structure they were now approaching. Wraparound porches with hand-hewn wooden railings graced both levels.

"Wow, this is quite a place," Jenna commented, sitting up a little straighter in her seat. "You and Sage grew up here?"

"Lucky, huh? Just think, all this land and these big wide-open spaces for two little boys to burn their energy off in. I had a great childhood."

It occurred to Dylan that she hadn't talked much about her own upbringing. Aside from knowing she was born in New Zealand and had, for the most part, grown up in the U.S., he still had a lot to find out about her.

They got out of the car and walked up to the entrance. Dylan pushed open the front door and guided Jenna inside, yelling out a "hello" as he did so. Footsteps sounded in the hall and an older woman came forward.

"Dylan! Great to see you!" She enveloped him in a huge hug.

"Aunt Marlene, I'd like you to meet Miss Jenna Montgomery. Jenna, this is my aunt, Marlene Lassiter."

"Mrs. Lassiter, I'm pleased to meet you."

"Oh, go on now, we don't stand on ceremony here. Call me Marlene and I'm going to call you Jenna. Head on through. I've still got a few things to see to in the kitchen. Hannah and Cassie are outside on the patio and Chance is fiddling with the grill, as if he thinks he knows what he's doing."

"No Logan today?" Dylan asked.

Marlene shook her head. "No, he called me to apologize and say he'd been called out of town for legal work for some high-profile corporate client but just between you and me I think he's ducked away to avoid the wedding planning." She finished with a wink and a sparkle in her eyes that took the sting out of her words. "So, go on outside. They're waiting for you."

Jenna appeared to hold a little tighter to Dylan's hand. He guessed it was a bit overwhelming when you came here the first time. He looked around the house he'd grown up in. Maybe the second time, too. Out on the patio she seemed to relax a bit more. The expansive gardens stretched out before them.

"Is that a pond?" Jenna asked.

"It's a saltwater pool designed to look like a pond. When Sage and I were younger we used to swing from a rope tied to a branch on that tree there—" he gestured to the limb in question "—and drop into the deep end."

"Wow, you really had it all, didn't you?" she said, almost to herself.

A little girl bounced toward them, her bright red hair hanging in disordered ringlets around her pretty face and her green eyes sparkling with mischief.

"You're my uncle Dylan, aren't you? But Mama says you're more like a cousin something-removed. What's that?"

"Cassie! Let Dylan and his guest say hello to the rest of us first, before you start bothering them," a woman's voice called from the patio.

Dylan watched as Chance's half sister, Hannah, rose from her seat and came over to greet them.

"Hi again," she said to him before turning to Jenna. "I'm Hannah Armstrong."

"Jenna Montgomery," she said. "Is that your daughter? She's adorable."

Hannah beamed with pride. "Yes, that's my little treasure. She's quite the character. Here, you leave Jenna with me and go and see what Chance is doing over by the grill."

Dylan gave Jenna a glance to see if she was comfortable with that. She inclined her head slightly.

"Sure, I'll be fine," she said, but he could see by the pallor of her cheeks that she was still a little nervous, as if, given the right provocation, she'd turn and run like hell back to Cheyenne.

"I'll say hi and then I'll be right back."

"It's okay," Hannah assured him in her gentle voice. "I won't bite."

Jenna let Hannah draw her over to where she'd been sitting a moment ago, and they relaxed in the late afternoon sun.

"I'm gonna help Grandma with the horse derves," Cassie announced importantly, before skipping back inside the house.

"Wow, she's full of energy, isn't she?" Jenna commented, her lips still pulled into a smile over the little girl's mispronunciation of *hors d'oeuvres*.

"Sure is. Has been like that from the day she was born. Never a dull moment with her around, and I wouldn't have it any other way."

There was a steely vein of pride running through Hannah's voice. One that made Jenna press her hand on her lower belly. Yes, that's how she felt, too. As scary and unknown as what lay before her was, she wouldn't have it any other way, either.

"It's so beautiful here," she remarked, looking around again, trying to take it all in.

"I know. When I first saw the place it totally blew me away."

"You didn't grow up here?"

"No, I'm from Boulder, Colorado. But I'm getting married next month and Cheyenne will be our permanent home after that. In the meantime, Cassie and I are staying here. She's loving having an uncle she can twist around her little finger, not to mention a Grandma who just adores her."

Jenna tried to put all that information together, but something was still out of sync in her mind. "Marlene's not your mom?"

"It's complicated. Chance and I share a dad," Hannah explained with a wistful smile. "But they've all been so welcoming since we found out about one another. Especially Marlene, which was so much more than I could have hoped for."

"They seem very tight-knit," Jenna observed, watching Dylan and Chance laughing together over something one of them had said.

"But inclusive at the same time. Don't worry." Hannah patted Jenna's hand. "I wondered what I'd be letting myself in for, but they made me welcome from the start. You'll fit right in."

Would she? Her heart yearned for stability; she'd created as much as she could herself by working hard and buying her own home. She was almost fanatical about establishing roots, about grounding herself in familiarity and routine after her younger years filled with instability. From what she saw here, the Lassiters were clearly just as invested in permanence.

"Here you are, ladies. Some icy cold lemonade for you, honey," Marlene said to Jenna as she returned, putting a tray with a couple of frosted pitchers and some fresh glasses on the table in front of her. "And margaritas for us."

Jenna felt uncomfortable. So they knew already that she was pregnant. She murmured her thanks and watched Cassie carry a tray with inch-high edges to Chase and Dylan.

"Used to be a time she'd serve me first," Hannah commented with a rueful smile. "But now it's all about her uncle."

"She might have him wrapped around her pinky," Marlene observed, "but it's mutual. It's good to have a child around here again. It's been too long since those boys were growing up."

The older woman turned to face Jenna, a warm glow lighting her hazel eyes. "How are you keeping with the baby, Jenna? Well, I hope?"

Jenna's upset that news of her pregnancy had preceded her must have been evident on her face.

"Oh, I'm sorry, hon. Is it supposed to be a secret? Chance told me and I just thought the whole family knew."

Jenna hastened to reassure her hostess. "No, really, it's okay. I'm just not used to people knowing just yet." She smiled to soften her words. "As to how I've been? I've been pretty lucky. A little nausea in the early stages but my main problem has been tiredness."

"You're in your second trimester now, aren't you?" Marlene asked. When she nodded, the other woman said, "You should notice you're feeling better again soon. This is where you get to experience all the fun of a pregnancy, without the sickness or the aches and pains. Is your family looking forward to the baby's arrival?"

Jenna squirmed a little. She was totally unused to someone being so inquisitive, though friendly. "I don't have any family locally," she settled on saying— unwilling to admit to anyone here that her father was doing time at the state penitentiary in Rawlins.

"Oh, you poor girl," Marlene clucked sympathetically. "Never mind. If you'll let us, we'd be glad to help you out. If you have any questions, anything at all, you just ask away."

"Thank you." Jenna blinked back the burn of tears at the kindness of Marlene's unexpected offer. Her eyes hazed over again and she lifted a hand to wipe at the moisture that began to spill.

"Don't you worry, honey," Marlene said softly as she handed Jenna a crisply laundered, lace-edged handkerchief. "We'll take good care of you."

Jenna wiped her eyes and fought to get her ridiculous emotions under control. She was a virtual stranger to these people. Yet because of one impulsive accident, they were prepared to open their hearts to her. She'd been so closed up, so reluctant to let anyone in, that she felt slightly off-kilter at the prospect of even thinking of accepting help and support. She didn't deserve this. Didn't deserve their trust or their generosity.

Even so, the idea of it dangled before her like a tantalizing, yet forbidden, fruit.

Nine

Dylan looked over to where the women were talking. Something tightened in his chest when he saw Jenna's expression and recognized the distress on her face. He went to step toward her, but was arrested by Chance's hand on his shoulder.

"Don't," his cousin said.

"She's upset. She needs me."

"Mom will look after her. Trust me. She'll have everything under control."

Dylan watched as Jenna recovered her usual poise. And as the women seemed to grow closer and enjoy one another's company, their laughter floated toward him on the light evening breeze.

"Do you want some more horse derves, Uncle Dylan?" Cassie asked from beside him, shifting her weight from one leg to the other.

"No, thank you," he replied, squatting down to her level. "But thank you for taking such great care of us. How about you offer some of those to the ladies?"

"Okay!" the little girl said brightly.

He watched as she strutted importantly to the table where the women sat. A sense of wonder stirred deep inside him. Would his kid be a boy or a girl? Would it one day be right here, playing on this patio like he had?

"So when did you knock her up?" Chance's voice interrupted his reverie.

Dylan's hackles rose. He didn't care for his cousin's turn of phrase. "I don't think that's any of your business."

"Of course it is. Sage thinks it isn't yours—that she's maybe pulling a fast one on you."

"Sage should keep his thoughts to himself," Dylan growled. "It's mine. And so is she."

His cousin nodded, clearly satisfied with that response. "You going to be a hands-on dad?"

"Every chance I get," Dylan replied emphatically.

Chance looked pensive. "I often wonder what life would have been like to have grown up with my own dad around longer, y'know?" His father had died when Chance was eight years old. He, too, knew what it was like to grow up without his natural father.

"Yeah. It's why I'm going to be there for my kid, through thick and thin."

"And Jenna? How does she feel about that?"

Dylan took a swig of his beer and rolled the brew over his tongue for a moment before swallowing. "She's coming around to the idea," he said with a grin.

Chance gave him a punch on the arm. "Thatta boy. Besides, with all you can offer, why would she refuse?"

"That's the thing. She doesn't seem to want what I can offer. She's fierce about her independence, and from what I can tell, she's worked hard for it. I just need to convince her that it's okay to share the load."

"Well, good luck with that. I'd rather rope a steer in a bad mood than try and convince a woman of anything."

"Good point," Dylan concurred, before gesturing to the platter of raw steak waiting to be cooked. "Hey, you going to do anything with those or are you waiting for them to cook themselves?"

The seriousness of their discussion broken, they turned to the matter of cooking the meat. But a niggling thought remained at the back of Dylan's mind. What if Jenna wouldn't let him in? What if she wouldn't share the load? What then? He knew he could use his power and his money to get what he wanted, but the very idea soured his stomach. No, he wanted her to come to him willingly and wholeheartedly. Not because she had to, not because she was being coerced. But because she wanted to as much as he wanted her.

It was late when he drove Jenna home. Dylan had fully expected her to want to leave soon after they'd enjoyed their meal, but it seemed that the longer she spent with his family, the more she wanted to stay. It made him begin to hope that she could see herself being a part of his own close circle. Part of his life.

"Thank you for taking me tonight. I really enjoyed it," she said softly.

"It was my pleasure. I'm glad you came."

"They're all so lovely. And Cassie's so sweet. I loved how she crawled into your lap after dinner and just fell asleep there."

He'd loved it, too. Had welcomed the little girl's trust in him. It had been a precious gift, and he'd missed the weight of her little body when Hannah had eventually lifted her and carted her off to bed. It made him yearn even more to be a father, to cradle a child of his own in his arms.

"Kids are special. No doubt about it."

Dylan drove onto Jenna's driveway and got out to walk her to her front door. He waited on the porch as she fitted her key in the lock, the breeze bringing a teasing hint of her fragrance toward him. Roses. She always carried that sweet scent on her. It suited her. The flower was so beautiful yet could be prickly at the same time.

She pushed the door open and hesitated a second or two. He saw her shoulders lift and then drop, as if she'd drawn in a deep breath.

"Jenna? You okay?"

She turned to face him. "Do you...?"

She bit her bottom lip, the action having the exact same effect on him as it had the other day. Fire licked along his veins as he waited for her to finish her sentence.

"Do you want to come in for a nightcap?"

Hell, yeah, a little voice all but screamed at the back of his mind. He didn't want tonight to end. She'd softened, somehow. Her defenses seemed lower than before. He pushed the screaming voice aside. He needed to tread softly. He certainly didn't want to scare her or damage the tentative closeness that had grown between them tonight.

"One more drink and I'll be over the limit to drive," he said quietly—asking her the important question without putting it into so many words. He'd go if that's what she wanted. He wouldn't be happy about it. But he'd go.

Jenna took a step closer to him and placed her hand on his chest. "Then perhaps you should stay."

His breath caught in his lungs. Could she feel his heart all but leap from his chest at her words? "Perhaps I should," he managed to reply, and hooked an arm around her waist.

They headed in together. He let her go as she walked around her sitting room, flicking on the occasional light.

"I'm not even sure what I have in the way of spirits, but I'm bound to have some wine. Would that be—?"

Her voice broke off as he caught her hand and drew her to him.

"I don't really want a drink, Jenna," he said, his voice a low rumble.

"You don't?"

"No, I just want you."

"Oh."

It was all she got time to say before he kissed her. The taste of her lips almost blew his head off and ignited the slow-burning embers within him to flaming, ravenous heat. His kiss was hungry, demanding, and to his delight she met his need with corresponding passion. Her hands slid upward, from his chest to his neck, then cupped the back of his head, not letting him break the kiss.

"Bedroom," he demanded against her mouth, not wanting to remove his lips from hers for even a second.

She pointed down the hallway. "At the end, on the right."

He scooped one arm behind her knees and the other behind her back and lifted her, holding her body against his. She snaked an arm around his shoulders and caressed his cheek with her free hand, as if she was as reluctant to break their connection, their kiss, as he. He covered the short distance down the hall and pushed the door open with his foot. Her bedroom was small, with minimal decoration. Simple in its design. A plainly covered bed took up most of the space, a solid plank of blond wood serving as a headboard.

Dylan let Jenna slide to her feet.

"I want to see you this time," he growled, moving away from her for the brief second it took to switch on the bedside lamp.

He turned back to her and reached to lift her loose-fitting tunic from her body. His mouth dried at the sight he revealed, his untaken breath burning in his chest. Her skin was smooth, with the lightest touch of summer in its tone. He let his gaze track down her throat, across her shoulders and to her breasts, which spilled from the lacy cups of her bra.

"I told you you were beautiful. I was wrong," he said, his voice thick with emotion. "You're so much more than that."

His hand reached out to trace a faint blue vein on her breast, and he heard her sharply indrawn breath. He followed the line to where it disappeared beneath the pale blue scalloped edge of her bra.

"I'm going to kiss you there," he promised, lifting his eyes to hers—his stomach clenching at the heat he saw burning back at him. "But first, I'm going to see all of you."

He took his time removing her sandals and slim-fitted capris until she had only her bra and panties left. Fine tremors quivered through her body as he let his hands drift up her arms to her shoulders. Her skin was so soft, and sweetly fragrant, and he trailed fine kisses along her shoulder and then up the side of her neck.

"Let me get the bed ready," she said as he nibbled on her earlobe, just as he'd imagined doing a few short days ago.

"It looks pretty damn ready to me," he said when she pulled away with a small laugh.

Still, he was happy to use the time she took turning down the comforter and tugging back the sheets to shuck off his clothing—something he managed with record speed. His erection strained at the cotton of his boxer briefs and he rubbed his hand down his aching flesh. Soon, he promised himself, soon. But first there were more important things to attend to. Such as examining the woman in front of him from head to foot. Getting to know what made her breathless with desire. Making her scream with pleasure such as she'd never experienced before.

Jenna lay down on the bed and held out a hand to him. He took it, stretching out next to her and marveling at how perfectly formed she was. He traced the curve of her collarbone again—such a delicate line—and followed his touch with the tip of his tongue. She rewarded him with a sigh of pleasure so he did it again, his tongue lingering in the hollow just at the base of her throat. Her pulse leaped against him, as avid and hungry as his own.

Dylan continued his voyage of discovery, his fingertips tingling as they met the swell of her breasts. He swept over their shape before letting his hand travel to her shoulders, slipping first one, then the other bra strap down, and reaching beneath her to unsnap the clasp.

"Should I be worried that you did that so easily?" Jenna teased, but then her voice ended on a gasp as he traced the pale blue line of her vein to where it collided with the dark pink distended nipple.

"Never," he said, before using the tip of his tongue to meet that pink tip.

She shuddered beneath him. "Do that again, please?"

"Your wish is my command," he promised, and did as she asked.

Her moan of delight drove a fierce spear of lust straight to his groin, but he forced himself to ignore it. To dwell instead on her pleasure, on her. He took his time with the rest of her body, lingering over her breasts, her ribs, her belly button, and then moving down to the small firm swell of her belly.

His hand hovered there and he willed the connection between them to go beyond skin, beyond sensation. His baby. His woman. His life. He pressed a kiss against her skin, his hands now skimming her panties, tracing the outside edge of the fabric where they met the top of her thighs. Her legs trembled at his touch, her pelvis thrusting upward toward him. He cupped her, marveling at the heat and dampness that collected at her core.

"Dylan, please!"

He pressed his palm against her, felt her shudder against him.

"You're teasing me. It's not fair," she cried, her voice a strangled sound.

"All's fair," he said easing her panties down her legs and punctuating his next words with firm kisses on her thighs, then the junction where they met. "In." Kiss. "Love." Kiss. "And." Kiss. "War."

His mouth found her center and he saw her hands knot into fists on the sheets as his tongue flicked against her glistening sex. The scent of her was driving him crazy. A delicious blend of rose and musk.

He couldn't stand it a second longer. He had to have her, be inside her, be one with her. He shoved his briefs down and settled between her legs, feeling her jolt as he nudged the blunt tip of his erection at her entrance. She lifted her hips in welcome and he slowly let himself be absorbed by the tight warm heat of her body. Slowly, so slowly, until he was buried in her. Until he was exactly where he needed to be.

His hips flexed and she met his movement with her own, her inner muscles holding and releasing him in time with their actions. Her irises darkened to near black, clouded with the fog of her desire. He tried to make it last, to make it even more special, but when her body began to pulse around his, when her eyes slid closed and she released a keening cry as her body shuddered toward its peak, he lost control—his hips pumping until he, too, reached his climax.

Lost in the power of wonder and emotion that swept over him, Dylan let his body take him on the ride as he crested wave after wave of pleasure. His entire frame shook with the force of what he'd just undergone—with the perfection of how it had felt. He rolled to one side and gathered Jenna against him, waiting for his heartbeat to return to anything approximating normal.

It was a long time before he could speak.

"I think we just proved our first time wasn't an aberration," he said with a huff of breath. He felt her chuckle ripple through her.

"Yes, I think we did."

He could hear the humor in her voice, humor mixed with a languid satisfaction that made him feel even better, knowing he'd contributed to her well-being. Everything was right in this moment. Perfect. He knew he'd never tire of this. Of the feeling of her in his arms, of the curve of her sweet bottom beneath his hand. Of this sense of connection he'd never shared with another woman.

He wanted this—forever, with her. It took all his self-restraint not to press her again to agree to marriage. To agree to committing to one another forever.

Deep down he knew she still had reservations. Understandable, given the short length of time they'd actually known one another. But they had the rest of their lives to discover all those finer points that kept a relationship interesting. What they shared was a gift beyond compare. He should know—he'd sought perfection wherever he went in whatever he did.

Jenna Montgomery was that perfection for him. He just needed to convince her of that fact.

Ten

Jenna could hear Dylan's heart racing beneath her ear, and her lips curved into a smile. He might be the CEO of the Lassiter Grill Corporation, he might be a world-renowned chef and playboy, but underneath it all he was still just a man. A pretty damn fine one, that was for sure. And, right now, he was hers.

Her man forever? She was beginning to believe it could be true. She'd loved spending time with him and his family this evening. Could she find the courage to reach out from behind her safe fortress and grasp what he offered? Only time would tell.

Dylan's fingers traced a lazy trail from her hip to her shoulders and back again, his touch setting off tiny shivers beneath her skin. She stretched beneath his touch, like a cat, almost purring.

"Tell me what you like," he asked softly. "This?" He firmed his touch. "Or this?"

"Hmm, let me take about the next twenty minutes or so to get back to you on that," she replied.

He laughed and the sound filled her heart with happiness.

"Twenty minutes? That's quite a commitment."

"It might be," she said, realizing that if she really wanted this—really wanted *him*—she needed to take the bull by the horns and open up to him.

But whenever he started talking about commitment it still struck a knell of fear inside her. He knew virtually nothing about her but the face she presented to him right here, right now. The person she was today was a far cry from the person she'd been eleven years ago.

Pretty much everything about Dylan and his life was an open book. Yes, he'd had sorrow in his life with the death of his parents and then his adoptive mother, and more recently, J.D. But with each loss, he'd had the advantage of family, of someone else willing to step up to the plate and fill that yearning hole in his life.

With the loss of his parents it had been J.D. and his wife, Ellie. With the death of Ellie, Jenna had learned tonight, Marlene had stepped into the breach to provide mothering to Dylan and his brother. What had Jenna ever had growing up, except a will for survival? That will had gotten her through her parents' arguments, their one-up-manship and then her mother's desertion.

It had gotten her through the news that her father was taking her to America, away from everything and everyone she'd ever known or allowed herself to anchor to.

Did she dare anchor herself to Dylan?

"You're thinking so hard I can just about hear the cogs turning in your brain," Dylan said teasingly. "Wanna share?"

She began to say no, but then realized that this was a perfect opportunity to give him some of her truths. What he did with it would define what happened between them in the future.

"I was just thinking about how different our lives were, growing up."

"How so?"

"You had such stability, such strength behind your

family. It's like everyone has a place and they fit there, y'know?"

"Uh-huh. It's not always a bed of roses but we get along pretty well."

"Pretty well?" she said, tweaking one of his nipples with a pinch that made him yelp.

"Okay, very well. But we work at it."

"That's part of what I mean," she said, smoothing her hand over his chest to soothe his injured flesh. "You do work at it, together. I guess I've never had that sense of community within a family. From what I know, my parents were both only children, and their parents died before I was born. It should have made them closer to one another, but instead it always felt like they were tearing each other apart."

"Doesn't sound comfortable, for them or for you."

"No, it wasn't. It was confusing, unstable. I never knew from one day to the next if they'd be happy and loving or morose and picking a fight. When my mother left us, I almost felt a sense of relief, y'know? But by the same token I was distraught because she didn't take me, too. Dad said she felt like we were holding her back."

Dylan sighed. "That was unfair of him for saying it and, if it was true, of her for feeling it. You can't do that to a kid. Your job as a parent is to nurture, to support and love your children. Yes, that means putting your own needs last a lot of the time, but I reckon there's a time and a place for everything and everyone, and when your kids are young it's *their* time, *their* place."

Jenna closed her eyes as a swell of something rich and true buoyed up inside her. His words were so simple, yet they rang with such a deep certainty about what was right and wrong. Tenets she held dear to her own heart.

"Well, obviously they didn't feel that way."

"Do you stay in touch with your dad now?" Dylan asked.

Jenna shook her head. She didn't want to tell Dylan that her father would be locked up behind bars for at least another two years. He'd probably have been out on parole by now if the prison staff hadn't discovered he'd begun grooming wealthy widows for future cons during his computer time inside.

"No. We lead totally separate lives. To be honest, I don't want anything to do with him," she said emphatically.

"Will you tell him about the baby?"

"No. I don't want him anywhere near us."

"Family is family, Jen," Dylan said, still stroking her skin, his actions soothing the anger that had risen in her as they discussed her dad. "I wouldn't be where I am now without mine."

She laughed, but it was a bitter sound. "Nor would I. But I've learned the hard way that just because someone is family doesn't mean they have your best interests at heart. My foster mum gave me more care and stability than my parents ever did. Thanks to her, I've learned to do very well on my own and I like it that way. I work hard, and what I have is my own. Okay, so I can't provide luxuries like saltwater ponds with swinging ropes, or private jets and silver spoons. But I can provide what counts—stability and constancy in a loving home. I've set down roots here. I finally belong somewhere and I'll protect that, and my baby's right to that, with every last breath in my body if I have to."

Dylan was silent for a while, but then he spoke. "And do you see any room for me in that life of yours?"

She rolled on top of him, her legs tangling with his

and her hands on either side of his face as she rose up to kiss him.

"That depends," she said, pulling away so they were inches apart.

"On what?"

"On whether you plan to keep telling me what to do, or whether you want to be an equal partner in what happens in our baby's life."

Tiny twin frown lines appeared between his brows as he looked into her eyes. "I can do partnership," he said carefully. "But I'd rather do marriage."

This time, when he said it, it didn't send quite the same shaft of anxiety through her. Instead, she felt a sense of curiosity—a need to take his suggestion and examine it more closely instead of rejecting it out of hand.

"I'll think about it," she said, hardly believing it herself as the words fell from her lips.

"Thank you," he answered simply.

His strong, warm arms closed around her and she caught his lips again, letting herself and her fears go in his touch until once more they were lost in each other.

The air had grown cool around them and Dylan shifted to drag the covers up over their naked forms. Jenna had fallen asleep almost immediately after the second time they'd made love, but he'd continue to lie there turning over her words.

Her family had hurt her, had made her doubt and fear closeness. Chipping away at her barriers would take time and care. And love? Yes, and love. Love and dependability. Those had been the backbone of his upbringing. He wanted those attributes to be the backbone of his kid's upbringing, too, and to do that he needed to woo Jenna with those promises. He'd known all along that courting her would be a challenge. They'd done everything from back to front, for a start. But he'd get there, he decided as he finally drifted off to sleep. What he and Jenna had between them was far too important. Failure was not an option.

In the morning Dylan eased himself from the bed-sheets without disturbing her. Dragging on his jeans, he padded through to her kitchen to see what he could rustle up for breakfast. He eyed her appliances with interest. Everything was new and in near pristine condition. Either she was a fanatical housekeeper or she didn't do a great deal of cooking in here. From what she'd said about TV dinners, he suspected it was the latter.

He opened her fridge and confirmed that she didn't do a great deal of cooking. His brow furrowed as he considered his options. A quick check of the vegetable drawer revealed a red pepper that was just about past its best by date, and some fresh mushrooms. He made a sound of satisfaction. Further rummaging in the kitchen uncovered potatoes and onions in matching earthenware containers.

So, with these items combined with the eggs in the fridge, he could do a Spanish omelet with red pepper and a side of fried mushrooms. His mouth was already watering at the thought. But when it came to slicing the potatoes, he eyed Jenna's knives in despair and wished he was in his own kitchen with his quality steel blades honed to perfection. Still, he'd made do with worse, he thought, testing the blunt edge.

He fried the potato and onions together in a pan while he went to work slicing mushrooms and beating the eggs. By the time he was ready to turn the halved omelet onto two warmed plates he heard a sound in the hall.

"Good morning," he said as Jenna stumbled into the kitchen, wrapped in a fluffy long bathrobe.

She looked as though she'd forced herself awake. Her hair was mussed and her eyes had a sleepy look about them that almost made him abandon their breakfast and take her straight back to bed to wake her up properly.

"Good morning," she said as she went over to the fridge and grabbed a bottle of water and screwed off the cap. "Something smells good. Are you feeding me again?"

"Spanish omelet. You hungry?"

She groaned. "Hungry? I'm always hungry lately."

"Then," he said, scooping up the sliced mushrooms he'd fried in a little butter, and sharing them between their plates, "you'd better wrap yourself around this."

She gave him a puzzled look. "You did this?"

He waggled his fingers in front of her. "With my own fair hands."

"Did I actually have the ingredients or have you been out?"

He laughed. "You had everything here. I haven't left you for a moment."

Nor did he plan to for the rest of this weekend, or any of the time he had free until the official opening of the Grill next week.

"Hmm," she said, quickly setting the small table she had in the dining area and transferring their plates onto the table. "Maybe you should give me some lessons."

His mouth quirked in a smile. Lessons? Oh, yeah, he'd love to do that. His mind filled with the possibilities, starting with Jenna wearing an apron…and nothing else.

"Sure. Shall we start today?"

"I was kidding, but if you're serious…"

"I never kid about food."

"Okay, today would be fine."

"Good, I'll take you back to my place. We'll have more to work with there."

She returned his smile and he felt as though the sun had just risen again. "Thank you, I'd like that."

Dylan heard his phone beep. "Excuse me a second," he said, sliding it from his pocket and checking the display.

It was a message from Felicity Sinclair, Lassiter Media's queen of PR, confirming her arrival in Cheyenne tomorrow morning. He tapped in a quick acknowledgment and turned his attention back to Jenna.

"Sorry, work," he said by way of explanation.

"Do you always work on weekends?"

He shrugged. "When it's necessary. With the Grill opening next week everything has become more time sensitive. That was just a text from our PR executive. She's flying in tomorrow. I'll bring her by your store and introduce you."

"That'd be nice. Hopefully, she can make sure that Connell's Floral Design's logo is featured prominently in your advertising," she said with a cheeky smile.

Jenna leaned forward as she scooped up a mouthful of omelet, her action making her robe gape open enough to give him a glimpse of one pink-tipped breast. Any thoughts of work and the people associated with it flew from his mind as he allowed his gaze to drift over her. She continued eating, oblivious to his perusal, until her plate was empty and she lifted her attention to him—and realized just what had caught his attention.

Her eyes darkened, as they had last night, and her cheeks became tinged with pink.

"Not hungry?" she asked, her voice a little husky.

"Starving," he replied, putting his fork down and pushing his plate away.

He eased from his chair, dropping to his knees and

sliding one hand inside her robe to cup her breast. Her nipple instantly tightened against his palm.

"Ah, now I see why you're feeding me so well," Jenna said, drawing in a deep breath. "You want to keep my energy levels up."

"Among other things," he drawled, letting his thumb graze back and forth over the taut nub that just begged him to take it in his mouth.

Never a man to ignore his instincts, Dylan did just that. Jenna's fingers tunneled through his hair, holding him to her as he nibbled and sucked her flesh.

"Well, it's a good thing I've eaten then," Jenna managed to say before he pushed aside her robe and lavished her other breast with equal attention. "Because I have a feeling I'm going to need the extra calories."

"Them and more," he murmured against her skin.

They didn't get out to his place until well after lunchtime and by then they were both famished again, for each other and for more sustenance. How they even made it into his high-tech kitchen bemused him, when all he wanted to do was take Jenna to the dizzying heights they'd shared, over and over again.

Instead, he supervised her as she put together a simple lunch for them both. Jenna surveyed the assembled ingredients on the island in the center of the kitchen.

"You always buy this extensively from the grocery store?" she commented as she tore up some romaine lettuce and threw it into a bowl.

"When I'm in the mood for Greek salad, yeah. What's wrong? Didn't your family ever cook?"

As soon as the words were out of his mouth he wished them back again. He already knew talking about her fam-

ily created an invisible barrier between them, one he'd
unwittingly put back in place.

"I can remember baking cookies with my mom once
or twice when I was little, but aside from that, nothing
really. Dad was big on takeout, or eating out. He often
wasn't home for meals anyway, so I just learned to make
do."

It was what she didn't say that struck him. How old
had she been when she'd been left to fend for herself
come mealtimes? Dylan moved around the granite-
topped island and slid his arms around her waist, pulling her gently back against him.

"I'm sorry," he said, pressing a kiss against the back
of her neck. "I didn't mean to bring that up."

"It is what it is," she said, studiously concentrating
on slicing the red onion and then the red and green bell
peppers she'd laid out in a row on the countertop in front
of her.

"Here, do you want me to do that?" he offered, wanting to do anything to change the subject and shift her
focus to something else.

"Actually, no. I'm enjoying this. I never thought I
would, but it's true."

She flung him a smile over her shoulder and kept
chopping and slicing until the bowl was filled with the
earlier ingredients, together with tomatoes, olives and
cucumber. Her hand hesitated over the feta cheese.

"It's okay," Dylan said. "I checked. It's made from
pasteurized milk."

"Are you sure?"

"Hey, leave it out if you want to. It's not a food crime."
To save her the hassle, he swept the packet up and put
it back in the fridge, substituting it for a sliced cooked

chicken breast. "Use this instead. There's no reason why we can't play around with tradition."

"Thanks," she said. "I'm sorry, I just don't want to do anything that will potentially harm the baby. He or she is all I have."

She placed one hand on her belly and Dylan could see the love in her face. He put his hand over hers. "You have me now, too. I want you to remember that, because I'm not going anywhere, Jenna. Not unless you're coming with me."

Eleven

She wanted to believe him. With all her heart she wanted it to be true. But she'd heard such platitudes from her father's mouth all the years she'd spent with him. He'd used them with her and also with his many lady friends. He'd always made it sound so sincere, as if the words truly came from his heart, but they'd come from a place far more closely associated with his wallet.

"Seeing is believing," Jenna said, trying to keep her words light. But she knew they'd struck to Dylan's core.

"You don't believe me?"

He reached to take the knife from her and turned her to face him. His hands framed her face and forced her to maintain eye contact with him.

"I didn't say that, exactly," she hedged, knowing to the depth of her soul that she wanted to be certain of him, to be able to trust what he said without looking for an ulterior motive.

Still, aside from the baby, and obviously the incredible sexual chemistry they shared, what else was there? A marriage took so much more than those two things. Her parents had been the perfect example of that. A marriage needed commitment, togetherness and mutual minds. What motive could he have to want to be with her? It wasn't as if she had something he needed. He had it all and then some.

"Jenna, I meant what I said. Yes, I know we haven't known each other all that long and, yes, we've gone at this all the wrong way. If I could, I'd turn back the clock and take the time to woo you, to prove that you can rely on me. Something brought us together, I firmly believe that. And we're meant to be, Jenna."

"I wish it could be that easy." She sighed.

"It can be. If you just let it."

"I'm trying, Dylan, honestly I am. I…I want to trust you."

"Then that's progress. I'll take it. We're halfway there, right? C'mon, let's get this salad finished and I'll show you around the house."

The next morning Jenna was happily reflecting on her day with Dylan when Valerie knocked on her office door and popped her head in.

"You have visitors. Mr. Drop-Dead-Gorgeous and a woman who looks as if she walked straight off Rodeo Drive. They make a nice couple," Valerie said, closing the office door behind her as she returned to the showroom.

A couple? Jenna didn't think so, not after the very thorough loving Dylan had given her yesterday. But even so, she felt a twinge of jealousy and insecurity. This PR chick, whoever she was, was certainly more suited to Dylan's world than Jenna ever could be. And she'd lay odds that she didn't have any dark or shameful secrets lurking in her past, either. Insecurity made Jenna uncomfortable as she rose from her desk and checked her appearance in the mirror that hung on the back of her office door.

Well, there wasn't a hair out of place and her makeup hadn't disappeared since she'd lightly applied it this morning. There was nothing else to do but go out and face them.

Her heart skipped a double beat when she thought about seeing Dylan. He'd been so attentive yesterday and had made her feel so incredibly special. She wished she was the kind of person who could simply embrace that and not constantly read between the lines of everything he said and did for an ulterior motive.

There was another knock at her office door.

"Jenna?"

It was Dylan. She pasted a smile on her face and reached for the handle. She felt her heart thump as she saw him. He was all sartorial corporate elegance today, dressed in a charcoal-gray suit, white shirt and striped tie. Her eyes skimmed past him to the tall, slim, golden-haired woman who was examining some pink hollyhocks. No wonder Valerie thought they made a cute couple. With the woman's tailored suit and high heels— Louboutin by the looks of them—she and Dylan looked as if they'd stepped out of the pages of *Forbes Magazine*. Jenna tugged at the loose-fitting tunic she'd teamed with a pair of stretch pants this morning, and wished her wardrobe had extended to something a little sharper for this meeting.

"Good morning," she said as brightly as she could.

Dylan didn't waste a second. He surprised her by swooping down and planting his lips on hers. Jenna put her hand on his chest to steady herself as her blood instantly turned molten. Two seconds in his presence and she was already starry-eyed. Man, she was so gone.

"Now it's a good morning," he said with a smile that crinkled his eyes at the corners. He linked her arm through his and drew her to his side. "Come over and meet Fee."

As he mentioned the other woman's name, she lifted her head and smiled in Jenna's direction. She took a few steps toward them, her hand outstretched in greeting.

"Hi, I'm Felicity Sinclair, but call me Fee," she said warmly. "Are these your designs? They're fantastic," she said, gesturing to some of the more artistic pieces the store had on display.

"Yes, mine and Valerie's," Jenna said, feeling a little more charitable toward the newcomer.

"You'd be very popular back home. I wish we had someone like you doing the flowers for our offices and functions. Dylan tells me you've got everything under control for Saturday's opening?"

"Yes, would you like to see a mock-up of the table settings?"

The next twenty minutes passed swiftly as Jenna went over her plans for the floral displays at the restaurant. By the time they left she felt a whole lot more confident in herself and her ability to hold her own with women like Fee Sinclair.

Dylan whispered in her ear as they were leaving, "Ready for another cooking lesson tonight? I was thinking of something along the lines of dessert, maybe with chocolate sauce?"

Fire lit inside Jenna, flooding her limbs and making them instantly feel heavy and lethargic. Her cheeks flamed in turn, earning her a considering glance from Valerie.

"Sure, your place or mine?" she asked, keeping her voice low.

"How about your place. It's closer to here for you in case we oversleep in the morning."

She nodded, not trusting herself to speak. He kissed her again, taking her in a hard and swift embrace that promised everything, but left her hanging in a daze of sensual awareness that clouded her already foggy mind.

"See you after work," he said, ushering Fee from the store.

After the front door had closed, Valerie zoomed straight to her side.

"And just when were you going to let me in on the secret?" she demanded, waggling a playful finger in Jenna's direction.

"Secret?"

"You and Mr. Drop-Dead-Gorgeous. You never told me you were an item."

Jenna smiled. "An item?"

"Sweetie, I saw the way he looked at you." She fanned herself theatrically. "And the way he kissed you? Well, suffice to say it had my hormones racing, and it wasn't even me he was kissing!"

"We're friends, Valerie. Good friends," she amended.

"He's your baby's daddy, isn't he?"

Jenna felt her cheeks drain of color. Aside from Dylan, and obviously his family, no one else was supposed to know yet that she was pregnant.

"I've had four kids of my own, remember. I know the signs. Look, I can understand you wanting to keep it quiet, especially with him being a Lassiter and all," Valerie continued. "I just wanted to say, good on you, girl. You work so hard, it's about time you had a bit of play. If there's one thing life has taught me, it's to grab what's offered and make the most of every darn second. You never know what's around the corner."

Valerie's words continued to ring in Jenna's ears as she forced herself to focus on her work for the day. Was she being a fool for trying to play it safe with Dylan? For not jumping, boots and all, into a future together? She didn't doubt he'd take care of her, but did she want to be taken care of? She'd fought to be independent, to be able to stand on her own two feet. Did he accept her as an equal? She weighed the thoughts in her mind, along with the realization that she was learning to trust him, to accept who he was. Could she take that final step and agree to marry him?

"So, what did you think?" Dylan asked as he drove Fee back toward the restaurant.

"Of the designs or of Ms. Montgomery?" she asked with a twinkle in her eye.

"Both. Either. Hell, I don't care." Dylan laughed. "By the way, I'd like you to see that her store gets linked to the Grill in the advertising push over the next few days."

Fee raised her eyebrows but took out her planner and made some notes. "Sure, no problem. The floral work is going to be fantastic—a perfect complement to the opening and the restaurant in general. About Jenna—she seemed familiar to me for some reason. I can't figure out where from. I'm not sure if it's her face or her name."

"She did the flowers for Angelica's rehearsal dinner. Maybe that's where you remember her from," Dylan said offhandedly.

"No, I don't think it's that. Not to worry, it'll come to me soon enough."

At the restaurant Dylan found it difficult to remain focused. All he wanted to do was race back to Jenna's store and sneak her home. Fee kept him occupied for the better part of the day, though, walking him through a couple of interviews she'd scheduled for tomorrow, among other things, and by the time he left the restaurant he was itching to get to Jenna's.

He'd barely thrown the car into Park when the front

door opened and she stood on the porch, waiting for him. He couldn't hold back the smile of satisfaction that wreathed his face. So, she'd missed him today as much as he'd missed her. That was definitely a step in the right direction. He snagged the bag of groceries he'd picked up on the way over, and raced up the path, sweeping her into his arms and delivering a kiss that he hoped showed how much he'd looked forward to seeing her again.

When he set her back down she looked a little starry-eyed, but a stab of concern pierced him when he saw how pale she was.

"C'mon, let's get you inside and off your feet. You look as if you've been overdoing things today."

He shepherded her through to her living room and sat her down on the long sofa, making her laugh when he picked up her feet and swiveled her around so she was fully reclined.

"Dylan, don't. It's not necessary. I just had a full day, that's all."

"And now you can relax. I'm here."

He said the words with a quiet authority he didn't really feel. In fact, with Jenna, he was never too sure just how close he was to overstepping the mark. He wanted to take care of her, to lift her problems from her slender shoulders and onto his broader ones. Especially when he saw her looking like this.

Despite her protests, he noted that she didn't make an effort to move off the couch, so he took the groceries through to the kitchen and poured her a glass of water, bringing it back immediately.

"Did you get off your feet at all today?" he asked, sitting at the end of the sofa and picking up one of her feet in his strong hands.

He began to massage her arches, and smiled when she groaned in delight.

"Oh, that feels good," she said, effectively dodging his question. "I'm thinking of keeping you on if you can promise you'll do this for me every day after work."

"You only have to say the word and I'm yours," he answered.

"The word?"

"Yes. And in case you've forgotten, that would be a yes to the will-you-marry-me question."

He deliberately kept his tone light.

"Okay, duly noted, and I consider myself fully informed," she teased with a tired smile.

Dylan picked up her other foot and began to massage it, as well, watching as she let her eyelids drift closed. When he stopped she didn't even move, so he gently placed her foot back down on the sofa and rose to go and prepare their evening meal. It worried him that she was so tired. Was that normal? He needed to do some research or talk to a doctor or someone. Maybe Marlene could help, or Hannah. He made a mental note to call the ranch in the morning, and then eyed the ingredients he'd bought for dessert before deciding to put them away for another time.

He worked quickly and efficiently in Jenna's kitchen, combining ingredients to form the spinach and pesto stuffing for the plump, free-range chicken breasts he'd purchased. He placed them in a shallow glass casserole dish, on top of quartered red potatoes that he'd tossed in olive oil. Then he smothered the breasts with the leftover stuffing before placing the lid on the dish and sliding it into the oven.

Just as he turned back from the oven, Jenna's home phone began to ring. He cursed the noise it made and dived for the handset on the kitchen countertop, hoping he'd get it before the sound woke Jenna.

"Hello?"

"Um, hello. Have I dialed the right number? Is this Jenna Montgomery's house?"

Dylan recognized Valerie's voice from the store.

"Yes, it's Dylan Lassiter here. Jenna's resting."

"Oh, good. I was just calling to see if she's okay. She took a dizzy turn in the shop today, and while I tried to encourage her to head home early, she flat out refused. Tell her that I've arranged for someone to keep an eye on the kids for me, so I'll open up for her tomorrow, would you? She can come in a bit later."

Dylan promised to pass the message on and placed the phone back on its station. A dizzy spell? No wonder she'd been looking pale. Clearly, she was overdoing things. His gut twisted in frustration. He was in no position to tell her what to do, but every cell in his body urged him to take charge and to make it clear that her health, and that of her unborn baby, should take greater precedence over her work.

But he was beginning to understand what her work meant to her. Without the support of family, she'd grown up missing the markers of encouragement and success that most other kids enjoyed. He thought about what he'd had growing up, and how he'd had the luxury of traveling and finding his niche in the world. How he'd taken all that for granted.

There were still huge gaps in what he knew about Jenna's past, not least of which being how she'd gone from living with her father to living here in Cheyenne with Margaret Connell. Dylan could only hope that eventually she'd trust him enough to tell him everything, to help him know her that much better so he could prove to her that spending the rest of her life with him was the best thing she could do for them all.

"Was that the phone?"

Damn, the call had disturbed her. By his reckoning she'd had only about twenty minutes or so of sleep, and judging by the darkness that underscored her eyes, she needed a whole lot more than that.

"Yeah, it was Valerie. She phoned to check up on you and to say she'd open for you tomorrow."

"She doesn't need to do that. I'm perfectly capable of opening the store myself. She has four kids to juggle in the morning," Jenna protested. "It's why she starts later."

"Clearly, she's juggled them so she can help you out. Why didn't you tell me you weren't feeling well today?" he asked, coming back into the sitting room and parking himself on the sofa again.

He lifted her legs and positioned her feet in his lap. Jenna got a defensive look on her face.

"I felt fine. I'd been bending down and when I stood up I just got a little bit dizzy. That's all."

"Have you felt dizzy before?"

"No, never. Seriously, I'm fine. Please don't fuss."

"Maybe I want to fuss over you," he countered. "Maybe I think you need a little fussing in your life."

She gave him a reluctant smile. "Oh, you do, do you?"

"Tell me, when was the last time anyone paid attention to you, real attention of the spoiling variety?"

Her grin grew wider. "I think that would have been last night, in bed, when you—"

"That's not what I mean, and you know it. Jenna, sometimes it's okay to let someone into your life, to let them share the load. I want that someone to be me."

Her face grew serious again and for a while she was silent. When she spoke, her voice trembled ever so slightly. "I want that to be you, too. I just—"

He leaned over her and placed a finger on her lips. "No, don't justify anything. I'll take what you said and I'll hold on to that for now, okay? Remember, I'm not going anywhere. I'm right here for you, whether you think you need me or not."

Twelve

Jenna stretched against the sheets in Dylan's bed, relishing the decadent luxury of the high thread count cotton against her bare skin. Last night they'd been out to the Big Blue for a family dinner, where the Lassiters had celebrated Hannah's engagement to Logan Whittaker. Again she'd been struck by the genuine love and warmth shared within the family. Love and warmth that had included her.

The siren call of being a part of all of that, the whole family thing, was growing louder in her mind, especially when combined with Dylan's attentiveness to her since Monday. He'd remained true to his word and shared her load; to be more accurate, it felt as if he'd shouldered the whole thing. Jenna still found it hard to accept gracefully, but she was learning. God, how she was learning. He'd delivered breakfast in bed each morning before driving her to work, his argument being that he didn't want her to suffer a dizzy spell while driving. And he'd collected her at the end of each day, to return to his or her home for dinner and to sleep.

And sleep they had. He hadn't made love to her since last weekend, insisting instead that she rest, and somehow, cradled securely in his arms each night, she'd slept better than she ever had before. She'd been unable to argue in the face of his logic, and had promised to follow up with her doctor if she felt the slightest bit dizzy again.

It was a novelty being so thoroughly spoiled. She couldn't remember a time in her life when she'd ever felt so pampered.

Or so loved.

He might not actually say it in so many words, but with every meal, every gesture, Dylan was using his attentiveness and care to prove that he'd meant what he said about wanting to be there for her in everything. Maybe they really could make this work, she thought, stroking the small mound of her belly through the sheets. Maybe they really could be a family.

She looked up as Dylan appeared in the doorway to the bedroom. He looked so sexy in just a pair of drawstring pajama bottoms slung low on his hips. His jaw was unshaved and his hair disheveled, and she had never wanted a man more in her life than she wanted him right now.

"How are you feeling this morning?" he asked, putting the tray with her breakfast on a bedside table and sitting down on the bed next to her to kiss her good morning.

"Fantastic," she answered with a smile. She raised a hand to trace the muscles of his chest, letting her fingers drift low over his ridged abdomen until they teased at the waistband of his pants. "In fact, any better and I think I'd be dangerous."

"Dangerous, huh?" He smiled in return.

She nodded. "I think I should show you how dangerous. Actions always speak louder than words, don't you think?"

Jenna rose up onto her knees, letting the sheet fall away from her body and exposing her nakedness to his hungry gaze. The look on his face empowered her. He made her feel so beautiful, so sexy, so very much in love. The realization should have hit her like a blow, she thought, but it felt right to admit it. To play around with the idea in her mind and to accept that with Dylan she could let go of the rigid control she'd developed to direct her life.

She pushed him back down on the bed, tugging at the drawstring of his pants and pushing the fabric aside to expose him to her gaze, to her fingers, to her lips. Then she showed him, slowly and lovingly, just how much he'd come to mean to her—imbuing every caress, every stroke of her tongue, with all that she felt and all that she wanted for the future. Their future.

Afterward, as they lay side by side, spent, their heart rates slowly returning to normal, Jenna looked across at the man who'd inveigled his way behind her defenses and come to mean so very much to her.

"Yes," she said simply.

Dylan's eyes narrowed and he looked at her intently, rolling onto his side. "Yes? Is that what I think it means?"

She nodded, suddenly shy and a little bit scared. This was letting go of her last vestige of control. But it would be okay, wouldn't it? With Dylan?

He reached for her hand and linked his fingers through hers before drawing them to his lips and kissing her knuckles.

"Thank you," he said with a reverence that brought tears to her eyes.

"Do you think your family will be okay with it? I mean, we haven't known each other all that long."

"They'll be more than fine, don't you worry. I'd like to announce it soon, though. No more secrets. What about at the opening the day after tomorrow? Everyone who matters to us will be there. Okay?"

No more secrets. Yet she still held one very close to her

chest. One that might change the way he thought about her forever. What the hell should she do? Tell him, and hope like mad that it wouldn't make any difference? Or keep it hidden away where it would hopefully never see the light of day ever again? It was impossible to know, but at least she didn't have to make a decision right now. After all, hadn't she just made the biggest decision in her life by accepting Dylan's proposal?

There was a time and a place for everything, and right now was not the time for the past. Right now was all about the future.

She slowly nodded. "Okay."

"Then I'd like you to wear this."

He slid open a bedside drawer and removed a pale blue ring box. Jenna's heart raced in her chest. Was that what she thought it was? Dylan slowly lifted the lid and showed the contents to her. A giant solitaire diamond, set high on a band embedded with smaller diamonds, winked at her in the morning light.

"Dylan, are you sure?"

He lifted the ring from its cushion and reached for her left hand, sliding the ring firmly onto her finger.

"I've never been more sure of anything in my life."

Dylan glanced around the restaurant. It looked, in a word, *perfect*. Jenna and her weekend girl, Millie, had delivered the table centerpieces, and they'd just left after putting together the massive tiered floral design in the foyer. Jenna had come up with an idea to use three up-ended logs of different lengths, and cunningly secured them so they wouldn't fall over. Her colorful floral displays cascaded over the logs in a tumble of nature's beauty.

It had given him a new appreciation for her talent as a

floral designer, and made him realize there was so much more to her than simply her ability to tweak a few wild-flowers in a vase and make them look appealing. An ember of excitement burned deep inside him. He couldn't wait to announce to all the world tonight that she was his, that they were to be a family.

Today really was turning into the culmination of so many years of hard work, so many of his dreams. God, he missed J.D. and wished the old man could have been here to witness it all. He'd been at Dylan's side for the opening of each of their previous Grills. Dylan had to hope J.D. was here with him in spirit today. He would have been so proud.

"Dylan?"

Sage's voice interrupted him, dragging his attention back to the here and now. Dylan turned with a welcom-ing smile, surprised to see Sage here. But the serious ex-pression on his brother's face wiped his smile clean away.

"Problem?" he asked.

"Mind if I talk to you for a minute?"

"Sure, fire away."

"In private?"

Dylan looked around at the hive of activity that buzzed about them. Waitstaff scurried back and forth, checking that the tables were all set to perfection and that every glass glistened. Through the serving window a similar hum of commotion came from the kitchen. If they wanted privacy, they'd need to go into his office.

Once they were inside, Sage made a point of closing the door behind him.

"What is it?" Dylan asked, getting the distinct feeling that he wasn't going to like what he had to say.

"Look, I don't quite know how to begin this."

"How about at the beginning," he prompted.

Sage's expression was stony. He drew in a deep breath before speaking. "I got that report back."

"Report?"

"The investigation into Jenna."

Dylan's blood hit boiling point in an instant. "You had no right—!"

"I had every right, as it turns out," Sage interrupted. He shook the contents of a large envelope onto Dylan's desk.

"What's all this?" he demanded, even as his eyes skimmed the words on one of the sheets that had fanned out.

Thief of Hearts! a headline proclaimed. The story went on to detail the trail of heartbroken victims a scam artist had left in his wake across the length and breadth of the country. Dylan continued to skim the article until his eyes jolted to a halt on a name: James Montgomery.

"Just because this guy shares her surname doesn't mean there's any connection," Dylan said, even though he had the distinct impression he was now grasping at straws.

Jenna had said she didn't see her father anymore. No wonder, if he'd been caught, tried and incarcerated for perpetuating such calculated crimes against innocent and vulnerable women.

"Keep reading. You ought to know," Sage said.

A knock sounded at the door and Fee popped her head inside.

"Am I interrupting?"

"No," Sage said before Dylan could answer. "Come in. You need to know this in case there's any fallout tonight."

"Know what?" she asked, coming into the room and closing the door.

"It seems my little brother's girlfriend is not who she appears to be."

"You don't know that," Dylan argued.

"Don't be so quick to judge me, Dylan. There's one thing I do know. That baby she's carrying *is* most likely yours. My investigator couldn't turn up any dirt on her in all the time she's lived in Cheyenne. Which begs the question, why did she suddenly latch on to you? Did she plan to get pregnant all along?"

"You bast—!"

Dylan lurched closer to his brother, only to have Fee step in between them. She looked from one man to the other.

"Guys, this isn't going to get physical, is it? I'd rather not be forced to explain black eyes at the opening tonight."

Her words compelled Dylan to relax the fists he hadn't even realized he'd made.

"You overstepped the mark, Sage," he growled.

"Can you blame me for wanting to look out for you? Read the articles then make up your own mind."

Through the fury that clouded his thinking, his brother's concern for him filtered through.

"Fine," he agreed, his jaw clenched tight.

"I'll leave you to it. Fee, you might need to read those, too." As Dylan began to protest, Sage overrode him again. "If my guy could discover this information, bear in mind others could, too. People who might want to cause trouble."

After Sage turned and left, Fee let out an audible breath.

"Wow, that was intense. What's it all about?"

Dylan swallowed back the bitter taste that had risen in his throat. "Some information he has on Jenna."

"Jenna? Really? Should we…?" Her voice trailed off as if she wasn't sure if going any further would be stepping on his toes.

Dylan sighed. "Yeah, we should. Here," he thrust half the papers in her direction. "Read."

Dylan finished reading the article he'd already started, feeling a sense of anger rising against Jenna's father for his callous behavior toward the women involved. Many of them were widows, women who'd lost their husbands and had sought male companionship, even love, only to find their bank accounts emptied and a pile of debt left in his wake when Jenna's dad left them. Imagine if something like that had happened to his aunt Marlene? Anger welled inside Dylan like a boiling cauldron.

He resolutely picked up the next article. Daughter In On It? questioned the headline. A photo of Jenna, much younger than she was now and with her head shaven beneath a tight headscarf, dominated the page. Even though she couldn't have been older than fourteen or fifteen, her beauty was easily apparent—perhaps even more so as she'd had no hair, so that the picture highlighted her large brown eyes and sweet smile.

Dylan's anger burned into a glowing mass of molten rock as the facts were grimly detailed. Jenna's father, the so-called Thief of Hearts, had used this photo of her and created an online fund-raising profile, saying she was dying of cancer and that they'd needed funds for her treatment. Dylan could barely believe what was there in stark black-and-white. While it was never proved that Jenna was a willing accomplice, questions still remained as to the depth of her involvement in that specific scam, as well as what had happened to all the money her father had conned out of his targets.

The article further revealed that as a minor, under the

care of the state when her father was sent down, Jenna would be put into foster care. That certainly explained how she had arrived in Cheyenne and ended up under Margaret Connell's roof—even though Mrs. Connell had never been known to foster anyone before then. Dylan reached for the printed single page report that summarized the investigator's findings. It went into interesting details about her financials. She'd attended the University of Wyoming without incurring any student loans and she'd also used a large cash deposit when buying her own home. A business loan had helped her buy the florist business. On their own, he could understand and accept each point, but the report raised far more questions than it answered. Like, where had Jenna gotten the money to attend university and buy her house?

Dylan reread the paragraph of the second article that talked about the sum of money that had been donated toward Jenna's "treatment." It was a hefty sum, reflective of the good will that had been shown by their community, and then abused and stomped on by her father. Apparently, the fund had been augmented by a six-figure donation from the woman Jenna's father had been known to be seeing at the time. Somehow, though, before the full investigation into her father's behavior, all that money had been withdrawn from the account set up in Jenna's name, and no amount of investigation had been able to reveal what had happened to it.

By the time he and Fee had finished reading the papers, a worried frown creased the PR manager's brow.

"Do you want to can the Q&A this evening?" she asked. "It might be best."

"It would be a complete break in our usual format. Wouldn't it raise even more questions if we do that?"

Fee pursed her lips. "You're probably right. I guess

we'll just have to hope that we can steer off any awkward questions, though I have to admit, I'm worried. As Sage said, if he could get this information, so can anyone."

Again that sense of being duped hammered at the back of Dylan's mind. It was information he'd have discovered himself if he'd been more diligent. If he hadn't been so swift to see only what he'd wanted to see.

"Let's just deal with it if it arises. Jenna's involvement in her father's scams was conjecture only."

Even as he said it, he felt his own doubts rise in his throat to choke him. Fee worried at her bottom lip with her teeth as she scanned the papers one more time.

"Are you sure that's how you want to handle it? In fact, are you sure you even still want Jenna there tonight?"

No, he wasn't. What he wanted was answers from Jenna. Answers he should have had from her before now. The fact she'd hidden all this from him hurt at a level he didn't want to discuss right now.

"Again, that would probably raise more questions than if she wasn't there. So, yes, I'm sure," he said firmly.

"Okay, then. I'll see you tonight."

Fee rose and left the office. He'd go to Jenna right now, he decided. He had to talk to her, to ask her for the truth behind this whole story. Determined to have this out with her face-to-face, he started to rise from his chair.

A loud crash sounded out in the kitchen, and within seconds a rapid knocking started at his door.

"Chef! Chef! We have a problem!"

Dylan groaned out loud, knowing that whatever was happening outside was far more urgent than talking to Jenna right now. He had more than a problem, he thought, as he shot from his office and into the kitchen to deal with the latest crisis. He had potentially opened up his whole family to someone who could be an accomplished scammer. One to whom he'd be inextricably connected for the rest of his life through their child. One who'd inveigled her way into his heart so securely that even entertaining the suspicion that she'd been a willing accomplice in her father's scheme caused a physical pain in his chest.

Sage had cautioned him about racing into this full-on, and Dylan hadn't listened. Had he been thoroughly duped? Had her playing hard to get all been part of her act? He didn't want to believe it could be true, but a devil of rationality perched on his shoulder told him he needed to consider all his options before taking this any further. As far as he knew Jenna had lived an exemplary life here in Cheyenne. Finishing high school, attending college, working hard and buying a home and a business. On the surface, it all looked so perfect. Too perfect maybe?

"Chef! We need you."

The shout spurred him into action. Right now, the kitchen was his priority; unfortunately, just when it looked as if his life was jumping out of the frying pan and into the fire. Deep down, though, Dylan couldn't help feeling a sense of betrayal. The other night, when she'd finally accepted his proposal, they'd agreed—no more secrets. And if this wasn't a breach of that agreement, he didn't know what was.

Thirteen

Jenna stepped from the car Dylan had sent for her, her gown falling around her in a delicate swirl of fiery-orange. The halter neck and empire waistline drew attention away from her bump, although she doubted she'd be able to continue to hide it for much longer. She thumbed the diamond ring on her finger with a small smile. Once their engagement was public knowledge it would be okay to let the news of their baby leak out.

She ducked her head shyly as some of the assembled media took her photo as she walked toward the front door.

"Name please, miss?" the stylishly suited young man at the door asked, before referring to his clipboard and ushering her through when she'd told him.

Dylan was part of a receiving line in the entrance. She drank in the sight of him in a dark pinstripe suit that looked as if it had been tailored specifically for him.

He was hers. The idea filled her with a sense of completion she could hardly dare believe. She really was the luckiest woman on earth. After all she'd been through, he'd become her light in the darkness. Her true north.

He looked up and she beamed at him, covering the carpeted distance between them as quickly and gracefully as her high heels would allow.

"Dylan, this looks amazing!" she breathed as she reached his side and lifted her face for his kiss.

She was surprised when his lips just grazed her cheek, but put it down to the swell of people pressing behind her as they came through the main entrance.

"I won't take up your time," she said quickly. "I'll leave you to your duties."

"No, wait just a second." Dylan caught her by the hand and turned to the man beside him.

"Evan, could you look after Jenna for me? Just until I can get free, okay?"

"Sure, absolutely no problem whatsoever."

"Jenna," Dylan continued, "this is Evan McCain, CEO of Lassiter Media. He's come in from L.A. for this evening. You'll be in good hands."

Jenna had recognized the ex-fiancé of Dylan's sister, Angelica, the minute she'd walked in the door, and said as much.

"It's good to see you again, Evan. I'm glad you could make it," she added.

"I wouldn't have missed it for the world." He smiled, his hazel eyes crinkling at the corners. "So, shall we go and see what the waitstaff are serving on those ridiculously large trays they're carrying around? I don't know about you, but I'm starving."

He offered her his arm and Jenna took it with a smile. She glanced back at Dylan, who was watching her with that little frown between his brows.

"I'll be fine. Just looking forward to when you're free," she said with a small wave.

He gave her a nod and turned his attention to the next newcomers in the line, welcoming the mayor and his wife with his accomplished smile and polite patter. As Evan led her away toward the dining room, Jenna couldn't help but feel that something was amiss. Aside from getting the message, through Fee Sinclair, that he'd be sending a car for her instead of picking her up himself today, she'd not had a single call from him. That in itself had been unusual.

Still, she silently reasoned, he was under a lot of pressure for tonight. In her call, Fee had mentioned the accident one of his staff had suffered in the kitchen earlier today, and Jenna knew he'd stepped into the breach. Did that explain the undercurrent of tension she'd felt? She hoped that was all it was, and that once he knew everything was running smoothly for tonight he could relax.

There was a loud murmur of activity at the entrance and Jenna turned her head in time to see Angelica Lassiter arrive, accompanied by a striking man. Tall, with dark brown hair and eyes that appeared to miss nothing, he looked incredibly handsome and yet had an air of ruthlessness about him that set her on edge. On his arm, Angelica looked absolutely stunning. Her shoulder-length hair was swept up into an elegant chignon that exposed the delicate line of her neck.

Jenna could feel Evan's tension as he watched his ex-fiancée's entrance. "Him? Of all the people she could have come with, she chose him?" he muttered.

"Who is he? I don't think I've seen him around here before," Jenna said, allowing Evan to turn her away from the newcomers and toward a waitress carrying a tray of canapés.

"No, you wouldn't have. No disrespect to you, but you don't move in Jack Reed's exalted circles."

Jenna couldn't help but recognize the bitterness in his voice. Evan continued, "He's from L.A., and has a hard-earned reputation as a corporate raider—all of which makes me wonder why he's even here. Unless Angelica did this to deliberately annoy me."

Jenna's first instinct was to refute what Evan had said.

She'd met Angelica again at Hannah and Logan's engagement dinner, and Dylan's sister had been gracious and charming. She certainly hadn't struck Jenna as malicious, even though there was clearly some undercurrent between Evan and Angelica's date. But then a tiny voice reminded her of something Dylan had said several days ago, about how upset Angelica had been when her father had cut her out of Lassiter Media in his will, leaving the controlling share to Evan.

"Well," Jenna said quietly, "I guess whatever the reason, the best thing for now is to make do with my company and show her that you don't mind who she's shown up with."

"Make do? Having your company is far better than making do," he said with a charming smile that lit up his face. "I apologize if I made it sound any other way."

Jenna laughed, the sound drawing the attention of the newcomers—in particular Angelica, whose set expression and sharp-eyed glare at Evan showed she was about as happy seeing him here as he was in seeing Jack Reed at her side. A swell of people moved between them, breaking the moment, and Jenna felt a wave of relief sweep through her.

Evan led her through the room, circulating among the gathering guests. The crowd consisted of Lassiters and members of the local chamber of commerce, interspersed with a few celebrities and a smattering of media. Jenna received many compliments on her floral displays and, from the number of business cards she was given and was asked for, would be rushed off her feet with work in the coming weeks. Things were really looking up, she thought, as everyone was invited to take their seats.

Evan showed Jenna to a seat at a table near the large stone fireplace in the center of the restaurant. The placeholder next to hers showed Dylan would be seated on her right, and Evan slid into the chair at her left. It took some time for the room to settle into quiet and for everyone to be seated. The lighting dimmed until only a podium near the front was well lit. She smiled through the gloom as Marlene and her date, Walter Drake, whom Jenna had also met at Hannah and Logan's engagement dinner, sat down opposite her.

Dylan took the floor, introducing his new Lassiter Grill team with pride. Jenna squirmed with excitement. Any minute now he'd be closing up the official business and inviting her to join him to share their news—their happiness—with everyone assembled. It felt odd, after so many years of keeping her head down and struggling to remain unnoticed, to be looking forward to being the center of attention. But as she watched the man she loved with all her heart standing there in front of everyone, she knew she could do anything in this world as long as he was by her side.

She thumbed the engagement ring he'd given her two days ago, and felt a swell of love build inside. She'd never been happier than she was right at this moment.

Dylan wound up the formal section of the evening, thanking everyone for being there, and asked if there were any questions from the floor. He smoothly fielded a number of questions relating to the restaurant before the tone began to swing toward a more personal note.

"Dylan, you've been spending a lot of time in Cheyenne lately. Aside from the restaurant, is there something or some*one* else responsible for that?" one of the female reporters asked with a sugary sweet tone.

Dylan nodded his head. "I've been seeing someone, yes, that's true."

The same reporter asked, "Are you going to tell us who that someone is?"

Fee, standing slightly to one side of Dylan, whispered something in his ear. He nodded and addressed the reporter.

"Jenna Montgomery. Many of you will know her already. She's responsible for the stunning floral designs here tonight."

A prickle of unease crept across Jenna's skin. That was it? Nothing about their engagement? She thought tonight was when he'd wanted to make the announcement. To shout it, loud and proud, that they were getting married and having a family together.

A different voice, a man's this time, rang out.

"Is it true that Jenna Montgomery is pregnant with your child?"

How on earth had some journalist heard about the baby?

Dylan kept his composure. "That is true," he answered smoothly as if the news was of no consequence.

The same man persisted. "Are you and your family aware that the woman carrying your baby is the same Jenna Montgomery who faked terminal cancer to help her father swindle nearly a quarter million dollars from a fund set up in her name eleven years ago?" the reporter persisted.

The room exploded in an uproar. Jenna felt the world tilt and a sensation like icy cold water ran through her veins. Through the haze of terror in her mind she heard Dylan's voice asking for calm. As the room once more fell quiet, Jenna found herself—like pretty much everyone else there—hanging on a thread waiting to find out what he would say.

"Yes, I am aware of Jenna's past and of the unproved

charges against her." He paused and whispered something to Fee, who went immediately across the room to two men standing to the side in dark suits. Together with them, she walked toward the reporter who had asked the questions. Dylan turned his attention back to the assembly as the reporter was quietly ushered from the restaurant. "Now, if there are no more questions, let's enjoy dinner."

An eerie silence filled the room like a vacuum as all eyes turned to Jenna. Across the table, Marlene looked at her in concern, a question in her eyes that Jenna had no wish to answer right here and now—or ever, if it could have come to that. She wanted nothing more than to run, and glanced around the room for the nearest exit, feeling like a cornered creature with nowhere to hide. Beside Marlene, Sage Lassiter's eyes bored into her as if he could see right through her to the woman he'd thought she was all along.

Her gaze flittered past them all, frantic to find a compassionate face, but everyone simply looked at her in a blend of shock or accusation. Here she was, a viper in their midst. Someone they'd accepted, welcomed—someone they really shouldn't trust.

Eventually, she looked at Dylan, silently begging him to believe in her. To *know* that she had been an innocent party in all that had happened. She should have told him long before. Her silence now made her appear complicit. Finally, his eyes met hers and she felt every last glimmer of hope for a future together fade into nothing. In his gaze she saw no trace of the teasing lover who'd shared her nights, nor the conscientious and caring soul who'd paid such devoted attention to her this past week. No longer was he the man who'd determinedly suggested marriage and then cajoled her into love—into believing in a time ahead where they could be happy together, be *parents* together.

A shudder rippled through her body, numbness taking her over until it was a struggle to draw in a deep enough breath. This was her worst nightmare. Her darkest, most shameful secret had been exposed to everyone here. People she admired and had come to trust. People who had come to trust her. Now that trust was crushed to smithereens, her hard-won reputation scattered to the corners of the county. She'd truly thought she'd managed to put all that behind her, but now, well, nothing could ever be the same again.

Dylan's eyes flicked from hers to someone else nearby, and seconds later she heard Felicity Sinclair's voice in her ear.

"Come, let me take you home. This can't be good for you or for the baby," she said in her capable, no-nonsense manner.

"Th-thank you," Jenna said gratefully, rising to her feet as Dylan continued to field a melee of questions from the media who'd been asked to cover the opening.

Fee guided her past the beautifully dressed tables—tables Jenna had helped decorate herself, in excited preparation for tonight—and the accusatory stares of the people gathered here punctured her as though each one was a spear of loathing. She couldn't believe how her world had turned on a dime, from one filled with joy and expectations to one where the future once again appeared bleak and lonely.

It seemed like forever, but eventually they were at the front of the restaurant and out the main doors. Fee ushered her immediately into a waiting car. Jenna didn't even stop to wonder how the woman had arranged for the driver to be there so quickly. Instead, she sagged against the seat, locked in a cocoon of loss, as Fee slid into the seat beside her and instructed the man to take them to Jenna's home.

Fee's hand slipped into hers. "Take a deep breath, Jenna. And another. Okay? Leave it to Dylan. He'll take care of everything."

How could he take care of everything? Why would he even want to? Jenna squeezed her eyes shut, but his image still burned there, especially the look on his face just before Fee had led her from the restaurant. The numbness that encased her slowly began to recede—replaced instead by a tearing pain deep inside her chest.

"It's going to be okay," Fee soothed. "You're out of there now."

Sure, they were out of there, but nothing was ever going to be okay again. Jenna had seen the questions in Dylan's eyes, the hurt and mistrust that had replaced the warmth and the love she'd already grown accustomed to seeing in him. Inside she began to mourn what they would never be able to share again.

She should have known better than to hope, known better than to reach out and take what he'd offered her so tantalizingly. She thought about all she'd undoubtedly lost. His trust, their future, his family. She would miss it all. Would she ever be able to look at him again and not see the accusation in his eyes? The knowledge that, of all the things she'd shared with him, that piece of her past was the one she should have shared first?

A discreet buzz came from Fee's delicate evening bag and she slid out her phone.

"Yes, we're on our way to her house."

Jenna could make out a muffled male voice at the other end.

"She's okay, for now. I'll stay with her until you can

come, just to be sure." Fee popped her phone back into her bag. "Dylan will be over as soon as he can get away."

Jenna nodded, but knew it wouldn't make any difference. What they'd had would be gone now. A man like him—a family like theirs—didn't need the notoriety that being with someone like her would bring. She'd known that all along, and yet she'd foolishly dared to dream it could be different.

Now, she knew, it would never be.

Fourteen

Dylan parked at the curb outside Jenna's house, leaving the driveway clear for the limousine that remained parked in the drive. He nodded to the driver as he walked past and up to the front door.

Fee opened it before he could knock.

"How is she?" he asked, his voice tight.

"She went to lie down as soon as we got here. Do you want me to head back to the Grill now?"

"If you don't mind. I guess you've probably already worked out a strategy to cope with any fallout over tonight?"

Fee smiled. "Of course. Leave it to me. This will blow over, you know. It won't affect the Lassiter Grill Corporation. If anything, the notoriety might even be good for you."

It might not affect the company, but it certainly affected everything else that was important to him, he thought as he escorted Fee out to the limousine. He watched as it drove away, and then turned and went back inside Jenna's compact home.

She was standing in the living room when he got inside. He was shocked to see how her dark eyes stood out in her eerily pale face. She hadn't changed from the gown she'd been wearing tonight, and it looked crumpled. His eyes drifted over her graceful shoulders, over the fullness of her breasts and lower, to where his baby nestled inside her. His gut twisted.

"Are you all right?" he asked, concern for her and the baby uppermost in his mind.

"A bit upset," she said, her hand fluttering to her belly. She gave a humorless laugh. "Actually, a lot upset."

He wasn't surprised. It had been a shock for him, too. First of all to discover that secret in her past, and then to have it laid out in front of everyone at the opening tonight.

Why had she kept it hidden from him? She could have told him at any time over the past few days, especially once she'd agreed to plan a future together. Did she honestly think that if she was an innocent party, he'd have felt any differently about her? Hell, she'd been so young she *had* to be innocent. Even if she'd participated in the scam, surely she would have been compelled to do so by the one person who was supposed to have been taking care of her.

Unless the real answer was all too damning. In general, people didn't hide the truth—which left an alternative that Dylan found distinctly unpalatable.

"It is true?" he asked. Everything depended on her answer.

"What part, exactly?"

He bit back the frustration that threatened to overwhelm him. How could she be flip about this? How could she continue to avoid telling him what he needed to know?

"All of it? Any of it?" He bit out the questions.

"There is some truth to it," she said softly, ducking her head.

"So you were involved."

Something passed across her face, something he couldn't quite define.

"Yes," she said, lifting her chin and meeting his scrutiny. "I was involved, but not voluntarily. I didn't know what my father was doing."

Could he believe her? He wanted to, but all the evidence, especially her silence on this very matter, suggested he shouldn't.

And it still didn't answer the question why she hadn't told him.

"What about me?" he asked.

"What do you mean?"

"What am I to you?"

"Dylan!" She sped across the carpet to stand directly in front of him, placing a hand on his chest. "You know what you are to me. You're my lover, the man I want to marry. You're the father of my baby. The man I love."

It sounded so sincere, and yet there were still shadows in her eyes. Truths that couldn't be told because maybe they weren't truths, after all. The questions that had been tumbling around in his mind all day were as irrational now as they'd seemed when they'd first evolved in his brain. Yet they still spewed forth from his mouth before he could have time to weigh them properly.

"Did I come across to you as an easy mark? Is that what it was? Did you see me at the rehearsal dinner setup and target me then? Or maybe the idea came to you later, when you discovered you were pregnant. Was that it?"

He saw her flinch beneath his onslaught. Felt her pull her hand away from his chest, and in its place felt coldness invade that part of him where his heart had beat steadily for her.

"I can't believe you'd think that of me," she said, her eyes wide with horror.

"Seriously, Jenna? We agreed, only two nights ago, no more secrets. What am I supposed to think?"

She stiffened her shoulders. "I can't tell you what to think. Look, perhaps it would be in the best interests of everyone concerned, especially your family and the Lassiter brand, if we didn't see one another again. I won't stand in your way when it comes to access to the baby, I promise you that. It's what I expected to do from the first, anyway."

She took one step back, then another, her fingers frantically working off the engagement ring he'd chosen with all the love he carried for her in his heart. She dropped the ring onto the occasional table beside her.

"Take it," she said bluntly, determination overlaying the anguish that still reflected in her eyes. "Just take it. I don't want it anymore."

He looked at the ring sitting on the table—its beauty an empty symbol of all his hopes. He scooped it up and put it in his suit pocket and turned and walked away.

"Fine. Since you still can't be honest with me, I'll go," he said bitterly. But nothing was fine at all. At the door he hesitated and turned back to face her. "You know what the worst thing about all of this is?"

She stared back at him, mute.

"The worst thing is that you wouldn't trust me enough to tell me the truth. I love you, Jenna. I really thought you'd learned to love me in return. Last chance. Tell me the truth."

She shook her head, her arms wrapping around her body, her cheeks glistening with the tears that ran freely down her face. Every instinct in his body urged him to go to her, to take her in his arms and to tell her that they could still work this out. That everything would be okay.

"Please," she said, her voice thick and choked. "Let yourself out."

She wheeled on her feet and fled down the hallway toward her bedroom. A second later he heard the door slam in finality. Raw pain, the likes of which he'd never known before, clawed viciously through him. Somehow he managed to walk out the door and get to his SUV. He sat there in the dark, staring at her house for a full five minutes, before starting the car and driving away.

Anger bubbled up from beneath his agony. Why couldn't she just tell him? Why couldn't she share that part of her that had now effectively driven them apart? Dammit, she'd chosen doing what was right for his family—even the Lassiter brand—over sharing the truth with him. What about his feelings? Didn't she care about them? Didn't she care that she'd let them both down?

Somehow he drove back to the restaurant, where the opening night party was still in full swing. He slid in through the rear entrance, but Sage caught him when he was in his office, about to put Jenna's ring in the safe.

"You all right?" his brother asked.

"No, I'm not all right," he growled, one hand swinging open the safe's door while the other closed in a fist around the ring in his pocket. It cut into his palm and he welcomed the pain. It matched how he felt inside. He flung a glance at his brother. "So, are you going to gloat? Tell me you were right all along?"

Sage shook his head. "You didn't see her face when that reporter threw that question at you. She looked as if her entire world had blown up."

"Her fabricated world, you mean," Dylan said bitterly.

"No," Sage said firmly. "Her real world. Maybe I was too hasty in showing you that report. Maybe we should have delved a bit deeper first. I agree," he said in response to his brother's snort of disgust, "it was my idea. But, Dylan, you didn't see how tonight affected her. Give it a few days. Go back to her. Talk it out."

He shook his head. "Not going to happen. She doesn't want to see me anymore."

He pulled his fist from his pocket and uncurled his fingers from around the ring, exposing the glittering piece before hurling it into the back of the safe and slamming the door shut.

"I didn't mean to hurt you, Dylan. You deserved to know the truth. But think on this. If she really was what those articles say she is, she'd still be wearing that ring."

Dylan weighed his brother's words. "You're probably right," he said with a sigh. "But until she's prepared to be open with me, I can't see us working this thing out. Besides, she'll probably never forgive me for what I said."

"What exactly did you say?"

"I asked her if I was her latest mark. I couldn't help it. It just came out. I was so mad that she'd kept something so important from me. Nothing about her life adds up, Sage. Nothing. Not unless she really was a part of her father's scheme and has been happily living off those proceeds all this time."

He didn't want to believe his own words, but without proof, without Jenna's own testimony, how could he think anything different?

Jenna walked on aching legs to her office to tally up the day's receipts. So much for today's cashless society, she thought, as she extracted the float to go back into the cash register, and then counted the notes to go to the bank the next morning.

She'd been beyond worried that after the disaster of Lassiter Grill's opening night, her business would slowly dwindle and die off. Instead, the opposite had been true. She'd barely been able to keep up with demand, and had been forced to increase her orders from the wholesalers. She and Valerie had been swamped working on special orders, and the foot traffic coming in through the front door had doubled over the previous week.

"Why don't you let me finish that up," Valerie offered as she entered the office. "You look dead on your feet."

"No, I'm halfway there already," Jenna insisted, even as a wave of weariness swept through her.

It wasn't the first time this week she'd felt weak and slightly disoriented. Considering she'd barely been able to force herself from bed each morning, or to eat or drink properly, it really was no wonder. Logically, she knew she had to look after herself, to look after the baby. But just now everything to do with herself fell into the "too hard" basket. She was glad they were crazy busy. At least at work she could get lost in the oblivion of one order to fill after another.

Valerie sat in the chair opposite Jenna's desk and studied her. "Have you heard from him yet?"

"What? No, I haven't. And I don't expect to, either."

"Never?" Valerie sounded regretful.

"Never, at least not directly," Jenna responded. She could hear the flatness in her voice and tried to inject some life back into it. "It's better that way."

"I don't see how. You're still pregnant with his baby. That takes two."

"Valerie, please. This week's hard enough as it is," Jenna implored her friend. "Can you just let it go?"

Valerie studied her from across the table. "Not when you look the way you do. I'm sorry, but I care about you. In fact, no. I'm not sorry. I *care* about you, Jenna. I've watched you go all the way from sweeping floors to taking this business over from Margaret and getting us to where we are today. You're bright, you're clever—but most of all you're honest. I know people have been saying things about you, and yes, I remember the stories about your dad from back when. It's shameful what he did to you and it's shameful that it's coming back to haunt you. You're not the person they said you are. The past belongs right there, in the past. I believe in you, Jenna. I just wanted you to know that."

Jenna gave the other woman a weak smile. "Thank you. I appreciate it."

"But it's not enough, is it? You still love him."

Jenna felt the all too familiar burn of tears in her eyes. She resolutely blinked them back, again. "That doesn't matter. What matters is this little person in here." She patted her tummy and was rewarded with a ripple of movement.

"Honey, trust me, it matters. You're killing yourself over this."

Of course it mattered. It mattered enough that barely a minute went by without her thinking of Dylan. Without seeing again and again the pain she'd inflicted on him and the disappointment that had been etched on his face before he'd left her on Saturday night. She drew in a deep breath. It would get better, eventually. She had to hold on to that thought.

Valerie persisted. "I think you should see him. Talk this out some more."

"He's gone back to L.A. At least that's what I heard."

"So pick up a telephone."

"No, really. It's over, Valerie. If I can accept that, I think you should, too. In fact, I'd appreciate it if you didn't mention it again."

Never would be too soon, Jenna thought as Valerie reluctantly agreed to her request.

"At least come to my house tonight for dinner. You can put up your feet. I'll make sure the kids wait on you and I'll cook you up one of my famous chicken casseroles."

"It sounds lovely, but to be honest, I'm beat. I just want to go home and go to bed."

"And have something to eat," Valerie added.

"Yes, yes, and have something to eat." Jenna gathered up the cash and checks and handed Valerie the float to put back in the cash register. "I'll do the banking on my way in tomorrow. Will you be okay to open up?"

"Sure. With my eldest and her best friend happy to mind the younger kids for a few extra dollars while they're on summer vacation, life's a whole lot less chaotic for me in the mornings. Don't rush in."

"I'll be here just after nine, I hope. We have another big day ahead."

"Which is exactly why I don't think you should be rushing around," Valerie teased with a laugh.

"Okay, okay. Don't you have enough mothering to do with your kids?"

"Hey, once a mother, always a mother."

Valerie went to put the spare cash in the register and then walked out the back with Jenna. "You take care tonight," her friend said, then got in her car and drove away with a cheerful wave.

Jenna watched her go with a wistful smile on her face. She'd never stopped to think all that much about Valerie's life beyond what she saw on the surface—married for sixteen years, with four great kids. Jenna was hit with a near overwhelming sense of envy for the simplicity of Valerie's world. For the security within it. She tightened her grip on the steering wheel and breathed in deep. She could do this. She'd been on her own for a long time now and she didn't need anyone else.

But even as she thought it, Dylan's face swam into her thoughts and with it a feeling of loss so devastating it made her head swim. She leaned back on the headrest and dragged in one breath after another until the woozy sensation left her. Then she turned on the ignition and put her car into gear, easing it out of the parking lot and onto the street, heading home.

She'd get through this. She just had to.

Fifteen

She was dragging her feet from the moment she got up the next morning. It was as if no matter how much time she spent in bed, or resting, it was never quite enough. Jenna surveyed the miserable offerings of food she had left in her fridge. Nothing worth eating for breakfast, she realized. She'd pick something up at a drive-through on the way to the store. She filled her traveling cup with drinking water, picked up her bag and went through to her garage.

Just as she pressed the garage door opener a wave of vertigo hit, and she put out a hand to the doorjamb to steady herself. It took about a full minute to pass.

"Pull yourself together," Jenna chastised herself out loud, adjusting her bag on her shoulder and stepping toward her car. "You ate a decentish meal last night. You can survive until after the bank."

She took a sip of her water, then another. There, she was feeling better already, she told herself, and walked the short distance to her car.

Driving to the bank, she felt fine. She found a parking spot close by and then went inside to wait for a free teller. Despite the early hour, it was busy for a Thursday. She hadn't been waiting terribly long before she felt the earth tilt beneath her feet once more.

"Not again," she muttered under her breath.

"What's that, miss?" said the older man in the line ahead of her.

"Oh, nothing, sorry."

"Are you sure? You look a bit—"

That was all Jenna heard before the blackness came out of nowhere to swallow her whole. She never even felt it when she hit the floor, nor did she hear the concerned cries from the people around her.

"You look like crap, man," Dylan's second in charge, Noel, said as he came into his office on Friday morning.

"Why, thank you," he replied in a voice loaded with sarcasm.

Truth was, he knew he looked like crap. Felt it, too. Since leaving Cheyenne he'd felt as if something—or more precisely, someone—was calling him back. He'd tried to tell himself he'd done all he could, that he'd overseen the opening to the best of his ability and that he'd left things in his executive chef's and restaurant manager's capable hands. Hell, he wouldn't have hired them if they weren't up to the job in the first place. It was time to pour himself back into what his job called for here in L.A.

Even so, his mind kept turning over that last conversation with Jenna, and with it, all the questions that remained unanswered between them. He'd done some more research and discovered that her father, James, had quite the reputation with the ladies. Exactly when he'd started fleecing them for every penny had been unclear, but when a couple of widows had begun comparing notes about their new beau over a game of bridge at their country club one afternoon, they'd seen and heard enough from one another to realize they were dating the same man.

After pressure from their families, they'd been the ones to bring the original complaints to the police, instigating the investigation into James Montgomery's habits. An inquiry that had unearthed a string of similarly swindled lovers in his past. Women who'd been too embarrassed to bring their situation to the attention of their families, let alone the authorities.

It made Dylan furious to think of so many innocents being duped by the charmer. A man whose first priority should have been the care and raising of his daughter. Dylan didn't understand how anyone could be so remiss in his duty to his own flesh and blood.

Speaking of *his* flesh and blood, he wondered how Jenna was doing. She'd be sixteen weeks along by now. When had she been due next for a scan? He huffed out a sigh and forced himself to relax his hand around the Montblanc pen he was strangling to death over the papers he was supposed to sign, and which Noel was waiting so patiently for.

"Your EA asked me to bring these in to you," Noel said, putting some pink message slips on Dylan's desk.

His eye scanned the papers, but it wasn't until he picked up the Cheyenne area code on one that he sat up and took notice. It wasn't like Chance to call him here at the office; his cousin usually called him direct on his cell phone, Dylan thought as he flourished his pen across the necessary pages and then passed the stack of documents over the desk to Noel.

"Was there anything else you needed from me today?" he asked the younger guy.

"No, I'm pretty sure we're up to date with these," he said, flicking through the pages. "I'll call you if anything arises from them."

"Thanks." Dylan nodded absently. He checked his cell

phone as he picked up the office handset to dial home. Two missed calls from Chance—yesterday. Whatever it was, it had to be urgent. His cousin picked up on the second ring, his voice gruff.

"Chance Lassiter."

"Hey, just the man I wanted to speak to. How come you're not working?"

"I wish I wasn't working. I'm going through the ranch accounts before handing them over to the accountant. But that's beside the point. Where have you been, man? I've been trying to get hold of you since yesterday."

"I had my phone on Do Not Disturb and forgot to change it back. What's up?"

"Have you heard about Jenna?"

Dylan stiffened in his chair. "Heard about her? Why? What's happened?"

"She collapsed in the bank yesterday morning. They had to rush her to the hospital."

"She collapsed? Do you know why?"

Dammit, he shouldn't have left Cheyenne. He shouldn't have walked away from his responsibilities to his unborn baby or to its mother.

"Mom called the hospital as soon as she heard, but they wouldn't give her any information other than to say Jenna was stable."

Stable was good, wasn't it, he consoled himself. At least she wasn't in serious or critical condition. "Has anyone tried to contact Jenna directly?"

"Sure. But her cell must be turned off. A woman called Valerie answered at the store, but she was about as forthcoming as a clam when Mom asked after Jenna."

Dylan mentally calculated what he had to complete today to be able to get back home to Cheyenne. Home. When had L.A. stopped being home for him? he wondered briefly, and then realized it never really had been. Sure, it was where he lived, but it wasn't where he belonged. Right now he belonged back in Cheyenne.

"I'll be there as soon as I can. Thanks for the heads-up, Chance."

"I knew you'd want to know. Hey, man. You're going to sort this out, aren't you? The rest of us don't care what happened to her in the past, or what she was involved in. We do care about who she is now, and she's going to be the mother of one of a new generation of Lassiters. She's one of us, whether she wants to be or not."

"Yeah, I'm going to sort this out," Dylan said, ending the call. *Somehow.*

But it was as if the world conspired to prevent him from getting to Cheyenne, from getting to Jenna and finding out what was wrong with her. He was as gnarly as a wildcat with a thorn in its paw by the time he dumped his remaining work onto Noel and instructed him that if anything else urgent came up, he'd have to handle it himself. To the younger guy's credit, he didn't so much as blink.

Dylan's executive assistant filled him in on the booking details for the flight she'd just managed to squeeze him onto at short notice. It would mean a stop in Denver, but at least he'd arrive in Cheyenne before midnight tonight. He cursed the fact that the company jet was down for routine maintenance. While he waited at the airport, he called the hospital and asked to be put through to Jenna, but was surprised to be told she'd already been discharged. That meant she had to be home, right?

In the departure lounge he tried her home phone number, but there was no reply. He tried her cell—again, no reply. He looked at his watch; her store would just about be closing. He dialed the number, only to hear the final boarding call for his flight. A security guard gave him a strange look as Dylan muttered a string of curses before grabbing his briefcase and heading to the gate. He'd have to stow his impatience and his concerns until he got to Wyoming and could see her for himself.

A delay in Denver saw his flight into Cheyenne land well after midnight. Dylan was chafing at the bit to drive straight to Jenna's house, but logic and reason told him that would be stupid. If she was home, she'd be sound asleep by now. The morning would have to suffice.

Once he arrived at his house Dylan shrugged out of his suit jacket and tore off his tie. He poured himself a generous measure of aged Scotch and threw himself into one of the large chairs in the living room. Sleep was the furthest thing from his mind right now. From the moment he'd received the news about Jenna, his primary focus had been on getting here. He hadn't really stopped to think about what he'd do when he arrived. Sure, he wanted to see for himself that she and the baby were okay, and he most definitely wanted to know what had caused the collapse that had sent her to the hospital in the first place. But what then? What came after that?

He still had questions to which she was the only one who held the answers. It had hurt him deeply when he learned she'd been holding back and made him say things he never would have under normal circumstances. But then again, their circumstances had never been normal, exactly, had they? That said, he'd been upfront about his desire to want to take care of her from the beginning. To build a future for her and their baby. Seeing her again, after their first encounter, had proved to him that their attraction was definitely not the kind of thing that crossed a person's path more than once in a lifetime. In fact, for many people, it never entered their life at all. He'd believed, down deep in his soul, that she was the one for him. Had that changed?

Aside from his natural concern for her, how did he feel now? Had knowing what lay in her past changed his emotions when it came to Jenna Montgomery? He took a sip of his whiskey and rolled the liquid around on his tongue before swallowing it. The answer to his question took a long time coming. No, he didn't love her any less. Sure, he was stung that she hadn't told him, but it didn't change how he felt about her at his core. He'd accused her of not trusting him with the full story about her past, but wasn't he just as bad not trusting her when she had told him she hadn't been knowingly involved in the cancer scam? Had he been so hurt by her withholding the truth that he hadn't even wanted to listen—had somehow wanted to punish her for that secret and therefore hadn't been prepared to believe her?

This past week had been hell without her. Without hearing the sound of her voice, the husky timbre of her laughter, the delicious hitch in her breathing when he kissed her intimately.

Could he imagine life without her? Hell, no, he couldn't. Every night since the opening he'd tried to see how his future would evolve without Jenna being an intrinsic part of it, and it had been a dark and harrowing place. He wanted her. More than that, he loved her with a passion so great he knew he could never settle for anyone else but her. Ever.

Which left him in a difficult position. He'd known from the start that their relationship was fragile, that it needed careful tending to bring it to its fullest and most exciting best. Had he crushed that tender seedling when he'd asked her if she'd thought him to be an easy mark? Could they revive the bond between them? She'd looked so battered, so bruised. He'd been so locked in his own anger and disbelief at what he'd perceived as disloyalty, not to mention dishonesty. He still wanted to know the truth, the full truth this time. They couldn't move forward until everything had been laid bare between them.

What was it she'd said, exactly? That she couldn't believe he'd think that of her. Somewhere along the line he'd earned her confidence, which was a far cry from where they'd been that day he'd swanned into Connell's Floral Design and back into her life. And, with a single comment, he'd destroyed it. But trust was a two way street. If she couldn't be 100 percent honest with him, too, then they didn't stand a chance.

He had his work cut out for him if he wanted to get her to open up to him fully, that was for sure. But he was driven to succeed in this, to surpass his success in everything else he'd wanted in his life to date. She'd said she wouldn't stand in his way with the baby, but he wasn't satisfied with that. He wanted them both.

What Chance had said resonated with Dylan. Whatever she'd done or been involved with in the past wasn't who she was now. Why should it matter? She was the mother of his baby. She was the woman who held his heart. That was all that counted. The rest, well, he'd deal with it one way or another, provided she'd let him. The morning couldn't come soon enough.

It was only ten o'clock and already Jenna was exhausted. Millie hadn't shown this morning, too hungover, if the garbled text message she'd sent had been anything to go by. Had Jenna ever been like that? she wondered. No, of course not. She'd been too busy trying to be invisible, yet invaluable at the same time.

A call to Valerie, to see if she could come in, even if

only for a couple of hours, had revealed that during the night she'd fallen victim to an apparently short-lived, but virulent, stomach virus that was ripping through their household. There was no way she'd come in and risk infecting Jenna, even if she could tear herself away from the bathroom right now.

Jenna had assured her tearful friend that she'd cope—after all, they'd completed most of the work for today's wedding client yesterday and by working back about three hours last night—but her head swam a little and she leaned against the counter, taking a swig of her water bottle and reaching for the salty snack the doctor had told her to introduce into her diet. She certainly didn't want a repeat of what had happened the day before last, and especially not at a time when she was on her own at the store. She'd had three bouquets to finish for the wedding today—now thankfully completed. With no Millie and with Valerie laid low with that stomach virus, it was all up to Jenna to handle those last-minute things, the things she'd counted on Millie helping her with so she wouldn't overdo it, she thought with a grimace. Not to mention walk-ins.

She heard the buzzer out front in the store. Ah, good, hopefully that'd be her wedding people in to pick up their table arrangements and the bouquets and boutonnieres. She forced a smile onto her face as she left the workroom.

Her smile faded the instant she saw who'd arrived.

"What are you doing here?" Dylan demanded. His face was a taut mask of control but she could see fire glinting in his eyes.

Jenna took a step back. "Where did you expect me to be? And what business is it of yours, anyway?"

"It's my business because that's my baby you're carrying. I went around to your place this morning, expecting to find you there, but you weren't."

"Well, obviously," she said drily, even as her heart rate picked up several beats at seeing him again.

"Why aren't you at home, resting?"

Oh, so he'd heard. She sighed.

"I just fainted, that's all." Jenna reached toward some roses she had on special in a tubular vase next to the cash register, and tore away a few damaged petals.

"Why? Have you been looking after yourself?"

"You're not my mother," she snapped. "I'm perfectly capable—"

"Don't give me that, Jenna," he growled. "I've seen inside your refrigerator. I know you don't cook for squat. Why were you hospitalized?"

"My blood pressure's a little low, that's all. I have to be careful not to let myself get dehydrated, and they recommended I up my salt intake. So you see, there's nothing to worry about."

"And the fall? You didn't hurt yourself?"

"No, and the baby's fine, too. Seriously, Dylan. I'm okay." Someone else came in through the front door. Ah, the father of the bride to pick up the flowers. "I'm also very busy, so if you'll excuse me?"

He didn't leave. Not through her discussion with her customer, nor when it came to helping the guy load the flowers into his van. Dylan even had the temerity to insist she stay in the store and sit down while he helped instead. She was seething by the time he came back inside.

"I don't need babying and I don't appreciate you coming in here telling me how to do my job."

"You're working far too hard. Aren't you supposed to have help here today? Where's Millie?"

"She couldn't make it, and...oh, there's a customer."

He waited while Jenna dealt with the woman. Then helped the client out to her car with the flowers she'd ordered.

"What do you mean, Millie couldn't make it?" he asked the second he and Jenna were alone again. "Don't you have backup?"

"Well, yes, sometimes Valerie will come for an extra day, but she's sick and she's already been doing most of the heavy stuff for me since my little incident."

"Little incident?"

Jenna could see he wasn't impressed by the terminology.

"Look, I fainted at the bank. The staff called an ambulance because that's their procedure. I was checked into the emergency department, and kept overnight for observation. I was rehydrated and then released in the morning with a set of instructions that I promise I've been following." *Mostly.*

It was as if he could hear her thoughts.

"Not completely, if I know you. What are your plans for lunch today?"

"I was just going to grab a sandwich—"

"How, when you can't leave the store unattended? How are you supposed to have a decent break if you don't have an assistant?"

"Well, I didn't know that she wouldn't be here until I got in this morning, did I?"

"Are you expecting any more customers today?"

"There are always a few walk-ins on a Saturday, but I have no more orders to fill."

"Good, then you won't mind me doing this."

He strode out back and she heard him locking the back door.

"What are you doing?" she asked.

"Get your bag."

"I won't do any such thing!"

"Fine. I'll do it myself." He shot through to her office and came out with her handbag slung over his shoulder. She'd have laughed at the sight he presented if she hadn't seen the look of absolute determination on his face.

"Dylan…" she started, but her words trailed away when he swept her up in his arms and carried her out the front door, hesitating only a second to turn the sign around to Closed. The door banged shut behind them.

"Key," he demanded, and she reached into her bag for her set, and while he still held her in his arms, turned the lock.

A group of people began to gather on the sidewalk.

"Hey, look at that! Isn't that Dylan Lassiter?"

"Yeah. Go, Dylan!"

To her chagrin, he flung them a beaming smile and began to walk toward his SUV, parked a few spaces down the street. As he went, the crowd grew larger, and began to applaud and cheer. Someone raced up to open the passenger door for him and another cheer rose into the air as he gently slid Jenna onto the passenger seat, before reaching around her to secure her seat belt.

Jenna was certain her cheeks were flaming. Dylan closed her door and marched resolutely around to the driver's side.

As he got into the car she flung him a murderous glance.

"This is kidnapping, you know."

"I know," he responded succinctly, right before he reached out to cup the back of her head and draw her to him.

Sixteen

His lips closed on hers with familiarity and yet with a sense of newness and wonder that tantalized and terrified her in equal proportions. On the sidewalk, the crowd went wild. Dylan broke away and reached for the ignition. For a second Jenna thought to protest once more, but the set of his jaw convinced her any argument would fall on deaf ears. She'd have to wait until he got her to wherever they were going.

It didn't take long to figure out. She recognized the route out to his home immediately.

"Dylan—" she started.

"Don't mess with me, Jenna. We'll talk when we're home."

He said it with such strength and distinctness it echoed in her mind. His home was in L.A. now, but from his tone it sounded as though he'd chosen the word quite deliberately. As if he meant to stay here. Her heart leaped in her chest even as her stomach dropped. The prospect of seeing him more often would be both torture and an illicit pleasure at the same time. She'd told him all along that she'd give him free access to their baby, so did this mean he meant to make his visits more frequent? Another more frightening thought occurred to her. Did he mean to get permanent custody? He had the funds at his disposal, and the family support.

She shoved the idea from her mind as quickly as it had bloomed there. He'd never once spoken along those lines. Why would he start now? Her thoughts flew back to last Saturday night at the opening—to the exact moment she'd felt her world come inexorably apart, like a dandelion destroyed in a powerful gust of wind. She simply couldn't go through all that again.

When they arrived at the house, he surprised her by parking in the garage rather than out front. She was even more surprised to see the red Cadillac gleaming under the overhead lights in the four-bay garage.

"You kept it?"

"I couldn't let it go," he answered simply as he lifted her from her seat and into his arms again. "A bit like you, really," he added cryptically.

He carried her inside to the casual family room off the massive kitchen, and put her down on a long L-shaped couch in the corner.

"Stay," he commanded, then wheeled around to the kitchen and went straight to the fridge, where he started pulling things out. In no time, he'd made a couple sandwiches on what smelled like freshly baked bread. He came back over to her and put a plate on her lap. "Eat."

She looked at him in annoyance, tempted to tell him where to stick his sandwich. But her mouth watered at the sight of it and she knew she needed to eat. Heck, she wanted to eat this layered concoction filled with freshness and flavor.

Once she'd finished, he took her plate, poured a glass of mineral water and handed it to her.

"Yeah, yeah, I know. Drink," she said, her voice dripping with sarcasm. This dictatorial side of Dylan was already starting to get old. "I am capable of taking care of myself, you know."

He just looked at her, his derision clear in those blue eyes that seemed to be able to stare straight through her. She couldn't hold his gaze. She might be capable of taking care of herself, but being capable and actually doing it had been two very different things.

"Things are going to change, Jenna," Dylan said, once she'd drained her glass and he'd taken it from her. "You are too important to me to leave either your health or the baby's to chance. You could have really hurt yourself in that fall, and what if it happens again?"

"It won't. I'm more aware of how I'm feeling now, and despite what you might think, I plan to take better care of myself." *It's just that everything else in the past two days has gotten in the way,* she added silently.

"Planning isn't good enough. You need more help if you're going to look after yourself properly."

"I know," she admitted. It was something she'd thought about a great deal this morning. One other person could make all the difference.

"So you'll hire more staff at the store."

Jenna's mind raced over the logistics of employing another full-time staff member—with wages, insurance and paperwork—and how that would upset her careful budget.

"At my expense—I insist on it," Dylan continued.

"Oh, no," she resisted firmly. What if he then decided to try to call all the shots when it came to her business? "Besides, it's not that easy to find a good florist. They don't just grow on trees, you know." The ridiculousness of that statement struck her at about the same time it struck him, and they both laughed. The sound lightened the mood, clearing the air as if by magic. Jenna let her barriers down. It *would* be great to hire another florist, someone who was innovative with design, yet didn't mind throwing together the traditional bouquets and arrangements that remained the backbone of her business.

"I'll look into it," she acceded.

"Thank you. I appreciate that you won't just get some walk-in off the street, and that in a business the size of yours, finding the right person might take some time. Can you get a temp until you find the right one? Do they even have temps for this kind of work?"

"I'll find out on Monday."

"I could do that for you," he offered.

"I said I'll do it and I will." She didn't want to relinquish an ounce of control to him if she could help it. This was her business and while, yes, he had a very valid point about her needing help, she would be the one looking for that help. Not him. Besides, didn't he have enough on his plate already? Jenna swung her feet to the floor and started to get up from the chair.

"Right, now that we have that sorted out, perhaps you could take me back to work."

"No."

Dylan stared back at her, his feet planted firmly on the floor and his arms crossed in front of him as if he was some kind of human barrier.

"Dylan, please. You've fed me, again. I've rested. Now I really need to get back."

"We need to talk."

"We've talked," she pointed out. "And I've agreed to get more help at the store. I thought—hoped—that would settle your concerns."

"On that score, yes. But there's a whole lot we didn't discuss last weekend that needs to come out in the open."

Jenna felt a fist close around her heart. So, they were back to her father. Would she never be free of his crimes?

Dylan reached out and took her hands in his. "I reacted

badly last Saturday. It hurt more than I wanted to admit when I learned you'd withheld stuff from me and in turn I hurt you back. I'm sorry for that. But I need to know everything. If you can be honest with me, Jenna, I believe we can work things out. Don't you want to at least try?"

She studied his beautiful face for a long time. He looked tired, with lines of strain around his eyes and those parallel creases between his brows that told her he was still worried, deep down. Could she do it? Could she share her shame with him and come out on the other side intact? There was only one way to find out.

"Okay," she said softly, dipping her head.

He let go of one hand to tip her chin back up again.

"Don't hide from me, Jenna. Don't ever hide."

Tears filled her eyes, but she blinked them back and drew strength instead from the reassurance in his voice.

"At first it was okay when Dad packed us up and brought us here to the States. We settled in Austin, Texas, where he was originally from. He met a lady, fell in love, but when it ended he just packed us up again, and off we went, somewhere else."

"It must have been hard, shifting around like that," Dylan sympathized.

"It was. I'd just get settled somewhere and the same thing would happen all over again." Jenna sighed. "I retreated into myself more and more, made friends less and less. His girlfriends started getting older and wealthier, and he started receiving more extravagant and expensive gifts from them. I would, too, because he always introduced them to me—maybe having me there in the background gave him some degree of respectability. They were usually nice to me, some more than others.

"One of them in particular, Lisa Fieldman, was especially lovely and she lasted the longest of all his girlfriends. There was a stage when I began to wonder—to even hope—they'd get married. That I'd have a mom again. She used to say she'd always wished for a daughter and that we'd do together very nicely.

"Lisa always had time for me and showed an interest in whatever I was doing. She even got my dad to come along to a school recital I was in when he'd never been to one before. I can still remember the big wink she gave me when I saw them in the audience. Lisa gave me a stock portfolio for my thirteenth birthday. She told me it would be something to fall back on—my 'rainy day fund.' I had no idea what that was and promptly forgot about it. I vaguely remember Dad trying to cajole her for control of it straightaway but she was adamant its management remain in the hands of her investment advisers. That was probably when Dad realized that she could see right through him. Despite that, I'm pretty sure she loved him, faults and all, but she wasn't a complete fool and kept a pretty tight rein on her finances. Of course, by the time the penny dropped for Dad and he realized he couldn't get any more out of Lisa, we moved on. It just about broke my heart. I'm pretty sure it broke hers."

Jenna paused a moment to swipe at her eyes.

"Your dad sounds like a real piece of work."

Jenna gave him a wry smile. "You have no idea. Anyway, I'd forgotten about the portfolio until I turned eighteen and some lawyer tracked me down to say it was mine to do with what I wanted. I couldn't believe it. Suddenly, I had funds that if I managed them carefully, could see me set up for life. I cashed in enough so I could get my degree without a student loan, and I kept working weekends at the store to meet my other expenses. I eventually sold off the balance a couple of years ago and used it toward buying my house."

She felt Dylan shift at her side and she gave him a piercing look. "You thought I'd somehow used the money my father swindled to buy my house, didn't you?"

He had the grace to appear shamefaced. "It was starting to look that way. The sums just didn't add up."

She nodded. "Yeah, I guess you're right. Anyway, I was able to use the house as collateral to borrow the money I needed to buy out Margaret when she was ready to retire. The repayments make things tight, but as long as I can keep afloat I'll get there in the end. The business will be all mine."

"That security is important to you," Dylan commented. "Owning your own home, your own business. Being answerable only to yourself."

Jenna nodded. "It became everything to me. It's the antithesis of what my life had been like up until my father was put in jail and I was sent here to Cheyenne to live."

"You were in Laramie when your father was investigated, weren't you? How did you end up here?"

Jenna rubbed at the mound of her belly absently. "Dad's arrest was national news and Lisa heard about it. Despite Dad ditching her the way he did and all that he'd put her through, she was still fond of me. Turned out she had a recently widowed college friend who lived here. That was Margaret. Lisa contacted her about taking me on. It was only supposed to be until I was eighteen, when I was theoretically supposed to be cut loose, but we got on well. I worked hard and she appreciated that. Plus, I also loved working with her and with flowers. We ended up being a natural fit. I have so much to be grateful to Lisa for, but I'm particularly grateful to her for using her influence to convince the authorities to send me to Margaret.

"Being here was a gift that I certainly wasn't going to

throw away. It gave me a chance to start over in a town where people barely knew of me. I hated every second of the publicity that surrounded my father's arrest. It was even worse when the media began to point a finger at me, saying I'd been complicit in his behavior. If I was guilty of anything, it was of ignorance. Maybe by the time I was fifteen I should have been asking questions about how he made so much money when he never appeared to work, but my head was filled with school and teenage stuff, so it never occurred to me to question any of it.

"One of my teachers got sick with cancer and the student council came up with the idea of a sponsored head shave to raise money to help her family out while she had treatment. When my dad saw me he was horrified at first. But then he took some pictures of me while I was visiting my teacher in the hospital. Without my knowledge or consent, he used those pictures to create a fake profile online, and used his imagination for the rest. It didn't take long for investigators to clear me of any involvement, but mud sticks and for me it stuck hard."

She thought back to that time when she'd been too afraid to leave the house and face the media assembled outside. Her father, then out on bail and awaiting the case to be brought before court, had simply taken it all in his stride, even laughing and joking with the reporters when he'd gone out. But for Jenna, who was still growing her hair back, every moment at school had become a trial by her peers, each day more unpleasant than the last.

"When Margaret placed me in school here I just did what I'd always done. Kept my head down and focused on my grades. By the time I attended the University of Wyoming people had begun to forget. Sure, I crossed paths with a couple of the kids I'd gone to school with in

Laramie, but time has a really good way of blurring the edges of people's memory."

Jenna studied Dylan's face again, and was grateful he'd listened without passing judgment. When given the chance, she'd grabbed the opportunity to forge a new life for herself, with both hands holding on tight. Sure, in hindsight she could see that her father had always believed he'd tried to do his best by her. That he'd obtained all those things under false pretenses was his cross to bear, not hers. Jenna knew that now. It didn't mean that she forgave him for it, but it was who he was.

"As to the money he raised, I have no idea where it is. He managed to hide it somewhere. No doubt he'll use it to seed his lifestyle when he gets out and the instant he does I hope the police will be back onto him. I'm sorry I didn't tell you all this before," she said softly. "I should never have accepted your proposal without doing so, but I guess a part of me was scared that you'd believe the worst of me when you knew."

"And then I did, didn't I?" he said ruefully. "Or at least it probably looked that way to you, huh?"

"In part. You have such a wonderful family, Dylan. I sullied them and your opening night at the Grill by bringing my life's ugliness into it."

"No, don't say that. What you went through made you who you are now. And we love you for it. All of us."

She searched his eyes to see if he was telling her what she thought, and hoped, he was saying. Sharing her past with him had made her feel lighter inside, as if it was no longer her burden to carry alone.

"Yes, Jenna. I do love you. I shouldn't have walked away from you last weekend. I was so angry and so hurt when I learned you'd kept such an important piece of yourself from me. I shouldn't have reacted the way I did.

You needed strength and support from me, and I didn't give it to you. But if you'll let me try again, that's what I'm offering you now.

"Everything, Jenna. My heart, my soul, my life. Knowing what you went through in your past just makes me want to create a better future with you, one for all three of us," he affirmed, placing his hand on her belly. "So I'm going to ask you again. Jenna Montgomery, will you marry me?"

Seventeen

Dylan's heart beat double time as he waited for her answer. He wanted this, her, the baby, more than anything he'd ever wanted his whole life. His happiness and his future hung now on Jenna's reply.

When it came, her simple *yes* was the most magical word he'd ever heard.

"I promise to make sure you never regret it," he vowed as he leaned forward and took her lips in a kiss that transcended every previous contact they'd ever had before. Nothing stood between them now. Their lives and their love were laid bare to one another.

"I know I never will, Dylan. You offer me so much, it makes me wonder what I offer you in return," she said uneasily as they broke apart.

"Everything," he said, and it was heartfelt. "I thought it was just a fluke, the way you made me feel the first day I met you, but you never left my thoughts. Through J.D. dying, through Angelica's wedding being called off... even when I was working hard on the Cheyenne Grill's opening, you were always there."

Dylan shifted on the couch so he could pull her into his lap, one arm wrapped around her while his other hand rested on the mound that resulted from their first meeting.

"I couldn't stop thinking about you, either," Jenna

admitted with a rueful smile. "It was…quite uncomfortable at times. I knew you were back in Cheyenne on and off, while the restaurant was being built. I guess I was a bit like a crazy teenager with a crush, hoping I'd get a glimpse of you. Your world, your background, is so different to mine. I convinced myself that you were unattainable for me, that our lives were too far apart and that I was happy not to hear from you or get in touch with you myself. But then I discovered I was pregnant, and it made me reassess everything. Made me wonder if you'd even be interested. After all, it's not like we got to know each other before we—"

"Shh," he said, pressing a short kiss to her lips. "So we didn't do things the conventional way. That doesn't mean we can't be as old-fashioned as we like, if we want to be, for the rest of our lives. Let's not wait to get married. I want us to be together, as husband and wife, as soon as we can."

"But what about where we're going to live? I—"

"I've been thinking about that. I have a strong team at my back. I can afford to work from here in Cheyenne, at least until the baby's born. After that, we can decide what we're going to do next, although I'd like to think I can make the move home permanent. I'd like to see our baby raised here, closer to my family's roots. So, what do you say? How does next Saturday sound?"

"Are you sure? That's a lot of organizing in a short period of time."

"We can do it, if we want to. I have contacts in the catering business," he said with a cheeky grin, "and I know someone who has a real way with flowers. If you're okay with it, I'd like to keep it small and invite family and close friends only. What do you think?"

She nodded. "That sounds perfect. Do you think we

could get married out at the Big Blue? It's an important part of your past and your family. I think it would be so special to be married there, where you grew up."

"I think that would be perfect," he said, kissing her again. "And I'm sure Chance and Marlene would be thrilled. So, shall we do it? I'll get the license on Monday and we can be married by the end of the week."

"I can't believe it's true, that it's really happening."

"Believe it, Jenna. Believe me. You are all I've ever wanted, you and our baby. I had some wonderful examples of love growing up. First my parents, and then J.D. and Ellie. Losing Aunt Ellie crushed J.D. He never stopped loving her until he drew his last breath.

"Even as a kid, I knew I wanted to know that kind of love with another person. I'm thirty-five years old, Jenna, I was beginning to think that kind of love wasn't out there for me, and God only knows I looked. I never expected to find it, to find you, right here under my nose in Cheyenne. And now that I have you, I'm never going to let you go."

"I'm going to hold you to that, Dylan Lassiter. Every day for the rest of your life," she promised, her eyes burning fiercely with her love.

"I can't wait."

It was a dazzling afternoon out at the Big Blue. As Dylan had expected, Marlene had taken the initiative and organized the wedding with the flair and efficiency he'd always known her to have. Strange how he'd thought he'd be wildly excited about today; instead, he was filled with a deep sense of rightness and calm. Everything he'd ever done to this point in time had led to this moment, this day, where he would declare his love for Jenna in front of their nearest and dearest.

He looked out the window of the second floor of the house and down toward the garden, where a hastily erected bower of flowers on the patio marked the spot where he and Jenna would become husband and wife very soon. A handful of waitstaff from the Grill circulated among the small gathering with trays of drinks and hors d'oeuvres, and he knew his executive chef had taken over Marlene's expansive kitchen to create a wedding supper that would rival anything he'd ever done before.

A knock sounded at the guest room door and his sister stepped inside. A smile wreathed Angelica's beautiful face, but he could see the concern in her eyes.

"Hey," she said, moving across the room to give him a quick hug.

"Hey, yourself," he answered. "I'm glad you could make it."

"Well, it was rather short notice, Dylan. Seriously," she teased, "a girl needs time to plan for these things."

"I figured if the bride could be ready in a week, our family and friends could, too."

"Good point," she said, stepping back and assessing him thoroughly. She flicked a tiny piece of lint off the lapel of his suit. "Speaking of which, this wedding is all rather sudden, don't you think? To be honest with you, I can't believe you're actually going through with it. Are you absolutely sure you're doing the right thing? It's no small step you're taking."

"I've never been more certain of anything in my life."

"Dylan, you don't have to marry her to be a father. You know that, don't you?" she pressed. "We hardly know anything about her."

"I know all that I need to know for now. I look forward to spending the rest of my life discovering the rest. As to not having to marry her—Angelica, I want to. I want her to be my wife more than I've wanted anything else in the world. It's a destination that I know, deep in here—" he thumped his chest "—we would have come to anyway. Having the baby, well, that just speeds it along."

"What if things go wrong?" she persisted. "Even when you think you know a person…"

Angelica's voice trailed off, leaving her bitterness and anger toward her ex-fiancé to hang in the air between them. Another knock at the door interrupted what Dylan was going to say, and Sage came into the room.

"You scrub up pretty well," he teased his younger brother.

"You don't look so bad yourself," Dylan replied, taking comfort in the usual banter.

"I never expected you'd beat me down the aisle," Sage commented lightly. But then his face grew more serious. "It's not too late to change your mind."

"Not you, too," Dylan groaned. "Look, guys, I appreciate the concern, but I know I'm doing the right thing. She's going to be one of us now. I'd like you to respect that. Can I have your promise you won't say anything about it again, please?"

Angelica and Sage each agreed, and the conversation turned to other matters.

Sage spoke first, directing his attention to their sister. "Since the three of us are together, I wanted to discuss the rumors that you're moving forward with contesting J.D.'s will."

"You're not still going ahead with that, are you?" Dylan asked.

"Of course I am," Angelica said with a stubborn look that the brothers knew all too well. She might have all her mother's beauty and grace, but deep down inside she was

J.D.'s daughter through and through. "As I recall, Sage, you were originally the one to suggest it."

His eyes reflected his frustration with her. "Yeah, but I also realized early on, and advised you, that continuing with the idea would prevent J.D.'s other wishes for inheritance from happening. Did you really want to see Marlene unable to live here? Or for any of the other bequests to be frozen while you battled this out? I thought you understood that it was more important to observe J.D.'s wishes in the end than to persist in something that's only going to cause bigger and bigger problems."

"Oh, sure." Angelica laughed, but the sound was insincere. "Nothing like the good ol' boys backslapping and agreeing to hush the little woman on her ideas, right? We all know Lassiter Media should have been mine. I did all the hard work. I picked up and carried on when Dad started to pull back from the day-to-day operations. Me! It's my baby and I want it back."

Dylan interrupted before things could get any more heated. Sage was right, but he could see where Angelica was coming from, even if he believed she was wrong. "I would have thought you'd want what's right for Lassiter Media. We all know that while we didn't agree with everything J.D. did, he was a brilliant businessman. He made his decision. Think of the wider picture, Angelica, if you even can anymore. You've become so dogged about this that your behavior is damaging the company. Is that what you want?"

She sighed and her shoulders sagged beneath the couture gown she wore. "No, it isn't what I want at all, but I have to fight for what's right. For what's *mine*."

Dylan put an arm around her. "We're going to have to

keep agreeing to disagree on this, Ange. This obsession isn't good for you, isn't good for any of us."

"That's easy for you to say," she retorted. "You got what you wanted."

"And I'd walk away from it all today if I knew that was what was best for the corporation."

The air was thick with the conflict until Angelica shook her head. "Let's not talk about this today, okay? We're here to celebrate you getting married."

The men grunted their assent, but Dylan knew the subject would not be forgotten. It was far too important to simply try and sweep under the rug. But for now, they could pretend there was nothing contentious simmering between them. He looked out the window once more, noting that the white folding chairs on the patio were filling with guests.

"Let's go do this," he said with a smile at his siblings.

Downstairs there was a hum of excitement in the air, yet it did little to ruffle the calm that wrapped around Dylan like a cloak. He'd spent every day in the past week looking forward to this moment, and finally it was here. Everything was coming right in his world, and he only hoped his sister could one day be as happy as he was.

Dylan took his place under the floral bower and smiled at the celebrant they'd booked to conduct the ceremony. Then he turned and looked down the aisle at the eager faces of the people he loved most in the world. All except for one, and she'd be coming from the house any moment now.

Jenna had elected to walk alone toward him, stating that she'd stood on her own two feet for so many years, she didn't need anyone to give her away. She was coming to this marriage freely and wholeheartedly. In response,

Dylan had elected not to have a best man, although they'd asked Sage and Valerie to be their official witnesses.

After a flurry of activity at the doors leading onto the patio, Marlene appeared with Cassie, who was dressed in mint-green organza and carried a basket of petals. Marlene flung Dylan a smile and gave him a thumbs-up. Until then, he hadn't realized he'd begun to feel nervous. No, it wasn't nerves, exactly, it was more anticipation. He couldn't help it; a big smile spread across his face.

Marlene took her seat and the music began. Cassie skipped her way down the aisle, throwing handfuls of petals on the ground, in the air and toward anyone who looked her way. Everyone was quietly laughing by the time she took her seat beside her mother.

And then silence fell upon them all as Jenna stood framed in the doorway. Dylan's breath caught in his chest as his eyes drank in the sight of her. Dressed in a simple white gown, with a broad satin sash under her breasts that lovingly contoured her slightly swollen belly, she looked radiantly beautiful. Her dark hair was swept up on her head, with tendrils drifting loose to caress the sides of her face and throat, and the diamond drop earrings he'd given her last night sparkled in the late afternoon sunlight. If he could have frozen this one moment in time forever, he would have. She was perfection, and she was about to be his.

Their gazes met and held as she began to walk slowly toward him, a smile on her face and her love for him beaming from her eyes. Then, finally, she was at his side, where she belonged for the rest of their lives.

The celebrant began to speak, and Dylan and Jenna made their responses, pledging their vows to one another. And Dylan knew, without a doubt in his heart, that he now had the family of his own he'd always wanted.

And as they turned to the assembly of guests as husband and wife, he looked at everyone's loving faces and knew this was the family he, Jenna and their baby deserved.

* * * * *

DYNASTIES: THE LASSITERS

Don't miss a single story!

THE BLACK SHEEP'S INHERITANCE
by Maureen Child
FROM SINGLE MOM TO SECRET HEIRESS
by Kristi Gold
EXPECTING THE CEO'S CHILD
by Yvonne Lindsay
LURED BY THE RICH RANCHER
by Kathie DeNosky
TAMING THE TAKEOVER TYCOON
by Robyn Grady
REUNITED WITH THE LASSITER BRIDE
by Barbara Dunlop

Available July 1, 2014

#2311 HER PREGNANCY SECRET
by Ann Major

Though he believes Bree is a gold digger, Michael nonetheless agrees to care for his brother's pregnant widow. But as duty turns to passion, what will he do when he discovers the shocking truth about her pregnancy?

#2312 LURED BY THE RICH RANCHER
Dynasties: The Lassiters • by Kathie DeNosky

Hired to restore the Lassiters' public image, Fee finds the perfect man in Chance Lassiter—for her campaign that is! Opposites attract when this city girl experiences firsthand the charms of the country—and a handsome cowboy.

#2313 THE SHEIKH'S SON
Billionaires and Babies • by Kristi Gold

Faced with raising the infant son he didn't know existed, Sheikh Mehdi marries for convenience. But the desirable Piper McAdams sees the man behind the devil-may-care sheikh, and for the first time, love may be within his grasp.

#2314 A TASTE OF TEMPTATION
Las Vegas Nights • by Cat Schield

Globe-trotting celebrity chef Ashton Croft meets his match in hotel executive Harper. But when a shocking family secret turns her life upside down, Ashton must decide if he wants to be her rock or a rolling stone.

#2315 MATCHED TO A BILLIONAIRE
Happily Ever After, Inc. • by Kat Cantrell

Needing a wife in name only, Leo Reynolds hires a matchmaker to find him the perfect partner—the sophisticated Daniella. But soon Leo wants to renegotiate the terms of their contract—in the bedroom!

#2316 WHEN OPPOSITES ATTRACT...
The Barrington Trilogy • by Jules Bennett

Working on location brings up painful memories as Hollywood hotshot Grant Carter is thrust into an equestrian world—jockey Tessa Barrington's world. But the innocent Tessa proves a temptation he'll risk everything for, even facing his traumatic past.

———————

YOU CAN FIND MORE INFORMATION ON UPCOMING HARLEQUIN® TITLES, FREE EXCERPTS AND MORE AT WWW.HARLEQUIN.COM.

HDCNM0614

REQUEST YOUR FREE BOOKS!
2 FREE NOVELS PLUS 2 FREE GIFTS!

H HARLEQUIN®

Desire

ALWAYS POWERFUL, PASSIONATE AND PROVOCATIVE

YES! Please send me 2 FREE Harlequin Desire® novels and my 2 FREE gifts (gifts are worth about $10). After receiving them, if I don't wish to receive any more books, I can return the shipping statement marked "cancel." If I don't cancel, I will receive 6 brand-new novels every month and be billed just $4.55 per book in the U.S. or $4.99 per book in Canada. That's a savings of at least 13% off the cover price! It's quite a bargain! Shipping and handling is just 50¢ per book in the U.S. and 75¢ per book in Canada.* I understand that accepting the 2 free books and gifts places me under no obligation to buy anything. I can always return a shipment and cancel at any time. Even if I never buy another book, the two free books and gifts are mine to keep forever.

225/326 HDN F4ZC

Name	(PLEASE PRINT)

Address	Apt. #

City	State/Prov.	Zip/Postal Code

Signature (if under 18, a parent or guardian must sign)

Mail to the Harlequin® Reader Service:
IN U.S.A.: P.O. Box 1867, Buffalo, NY 14240-1867
IN CANADA: P.O. Box 609, Fort Erie, Ontario L2A 5X3

Want to try two free books from another line?
Call 1-800-873-8635 or visit www.ReaderService.com.

* Terms and prices subject to change without notice. Prices do not include applicable taxes. Sales tax applicable in N.Y. Canadian residents will be charged applicable taxes. Offer not valid in Quebec. This offer is limited to one order per household. Not valid for current subscribers to Harlequin Desire books. All orders subject to credit approval. Credit or debit balances in a customer's account(s) may be offset by any other outstanding balance owed by or to the customer. Please allow 4 to 6 weeks for delivery. Offer available while quantities last.

Your Privacy—The Harlequin® Reader Service is committed to protecting your privacy. Our Privacy Policy is available online at www.ReaderService.com or upon request from the Harlequin Reader Service.

We make a portion of our mailing list available to reputable third parties that offer products we believe may interest you. If you prefer that we not exchange your name with third parties, or if you wish to clarify or modify your communication preferences, please visit us at www.ReaderService.com/consumerschoice or write to us at Harlequin Reader Service Preference Service, P.O. Box 9062, Buffalo, NY 14269. Include your complete name and address.

HD13R

"**W**ould you like to dance, Ms. Sinclair?"

She glanced at her uncomfortable-looking high heels.
"I...hadn't thought I would be dancing."

Laughing, Chance Lassiter bent down to whisper close
to her ear. "I'm from the school of stand in one place and
sway."

Her delightful laughter caused a warm feeling to spread
throughout his chest. "I think that's about all I'll be able to
do in these shoes anyway."

When she placed her soft hand in his and stood up to walk
out onto the dance floor with him, an electric current shot
straight up his arm. He wrapped his arms loosely around her
and smiled down at her upturned face.

"Chance, there's something I'd like to discuss with you,"
she said as they swayed back and forth.

"I'm all ears," he said, grinning.

"I'd like your help with my public relations campaign to
improve the Lassiters' image."

"Sure. I'll do whatever I can to help you out," he said,
drawing her a little closer. "What did you have in mind?"

"You're going to be the family spokesman for the PR campaign that I'm planning," she said, beaming.

Marveling at how beautiful she was, it took a moment for her words to register with him. He stopped swaying and stared down at her in disbelief. "You want me to do what?"

"I'm going to have you appear in all future advertising for Lassiter Media," she said, sounding extremely excited. "You'll be in the national television commercials, as well as…"

Chance silently ran through every cuss word he'd ever heard. He might be a Lassiter, but he wasn't as refined as the rest of the family. Instead of riding a desk in some corporate office, he was on the back of a horse every day herding cattle under the wide Wyoming sky. That was the way he liked it and the way he intended for things to stay. There was no way in hell he was going to be the family spokesman. And the sooner he could find a way to get that across to her, the better.

Don't miss
LURED BY THE RICH RANCHER
by Kathie DeNosky.

Available July 2014,
wherever Harlequin® Desire books are sold.